The Eye in the Forest

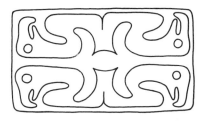

The Eye in the Forest

Mary Q. Steele and William O. Steele

E. P. DUTTON & CO., INC.   NEW YORK

The design motif that appears on the title page
and elsewhere is from *The Adena People, No. 2*, p. 101,
by William S. Webb and Raymond S. Baby. Reprinted
by courtesy of The Ohio Historical Society.

Map by Jeanyee Wong

LIBRARY OF CONGRESS CATALOGING IN PUBLICATION DATA

Steele, Mary Q. and William O.   The eye in the forest

SUMMARY: A young Adena Indian novitiate accompanies a party
led by his priest-teacher on the long and dangerous journey
in search of the sacred place where their tribe originated.

[1. Mound builders—Fiction]   I. Title
PZ7.S8146Ey   [Fic]   74-23768   ISBN 0-525-29510-0

Published simultaneously in Canada by Clarke,
Irwin & Company Limited, Toronto and Vancouver

Designed by Riki Levinson
Printed in the U.S.A.   First Edition
10 9 8 7 6 5 4 3 2 1

For Princess Corntassel

Curator of the SCH Collection
of Indian Artifacts, with many thanks
for her invaluable assistance—
and with love.

Holy Chant of the Adena People

Away from the Eye that closed
North went the sad Adena
Following the wings of the Sacred Eagle of Life
Carrying the holy slate tablets
Carrying the great skull bowl wherein the Dream Visions lie
Carrying the Two-Legged Sacred Breath
Across flat land where grass spread blue and rainbow
    springs danced
Across flat land where earth mouths blew out the dead air
    of the dark world below
Over the waters flowing bitter as tears
Across the everlasting hills
North where the Eagle goes
While above the thin child moon was born and swelled with
    living fire and died old and cold
That long the Adena followed
Till beyond the Crystal River the Great Eagle folded his
    wings and rested
There the Adena rested with him in the strange new earth-place
Rested till time to return south to the Eye in the Forest
    and live once again
Rested, waiting for the bright life to shine outward once
    again from the Eye in the Forest.

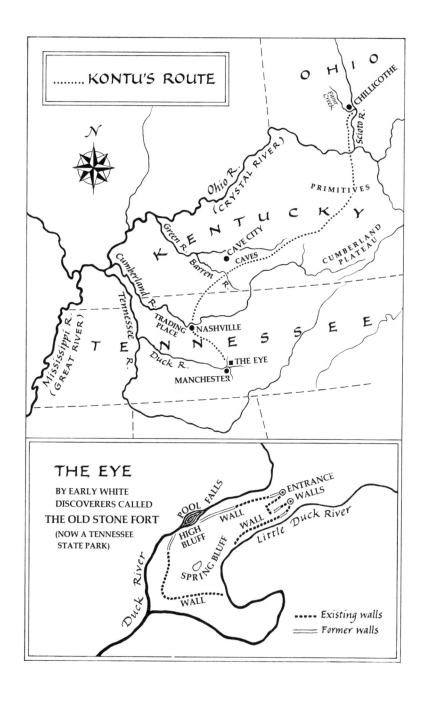

.... KONTU'S ROUTE

N

OHIO

Point Creek

CHILLICOTHE

Scioto R.

Ohio R. (CRYSTAL RIVER)

PRIMITIVES

K E N T U C K Y

Green R.

CAVE CITY

CAVES

CUMBERLAND PLATEAU

Barren R.

Cumberland R.

Tennessee R.

TRADING PLACE

NASHVILLE

T E N N E S S E E

Mississippi R. (GREAT RIVER)

Duck R.

THE EYE

MANCHESTER

THE EYE

BY EARLY WHITE
DISCOVERERS CALLED

THE OLD STONE FORT

(NOW A TENNESSEE
STATE PARK)

POOL FALLS

ENTRANCE
WALLS

WALL

WALL

Little Duck River

HIGH BLUFF

SPRING BLUFF

Duck River

WALL

••••• Existing walls
——— Former walls

Chapter One

Kontu climbed the ridge. He went slowly. He was in no particular hurry to reach the top. He had not much doubt what he would find when he got there.

He was right. When he stood at last on the crest and looked down, what lay before him was a green plain of treetops. The round tops of oaks, the pointed tops of poplars, the gaunt dark tops of a few pines. In the fading light it was the same view as last night, and the one before that. There was no end to these ridges and thick woods.

He stared across the valley to the next ridge. Beyond those rocky cliffs lay what? Another valley, filled with trees as a lake is filled with water. And beyond that? The Sacred Eye?

It was strange to be here, so far from home, so far from the familiar low hills and forests north of the Crystal River. They had traveled a long way, the four of them, Kontu and Yovo and the two warriors, Watota and Gunt. And how much farther they would have to go, no one could say. Not even Yovo, who knew everything because he was a priest and had lived a long time and seen much.

A dove called and another answered, softly, sadly, *roocoocoocoo.* Yovo had told Kontu what the doves were saying: They were saying, Mourn for those who have strayed from the right path and wander miserably in the dark; help them find their way once more.

Yovo was not sure what had happened so long ago when the Adena people lost their Eye in the Forest. He did not know whether they had strayed from the right path or simply been the victims of some evil-wisher. But Yovo did know that the Eye in the Forest was shut in sleep, waiting for the Adena to return. He did know that the Eye would not reveal itself to that other Adena priest and the young initiates and warriors who had gone with him.

"Our people came here through the forests and across the rivers and over the hills on their feet," Yovo said scornfully as they packed their sacred bundles in the village temple. "To seek the Eye by getting in boats and traveling down the water of the rivers is foolish. When you have journeyed away from a thing, you must journey back the same way, or you cannot find it."

Kontu sighed a little and looked again out across the treetops. It seemed right, it seemed wise to hear Yovo say it. And he had been glad when he was chosen to go with Yovo along the paths and through the trees. And yet—and yet, he would have liked to be with that other younger priest and his four initiates and six warriors in their boats. It would have been at least a merry voyage.

He was ashamed of his thoughts. They were not on this mission to enjoy themselves and make jokes and shove each other into the water and wrestle and tell lies around the fire at night. They were here to find the Eye in the Forest in order that the Adena people might be saved from death and terror and live once again in honor and decency. It was a solemn thing.

He turned around and started back through the rocks the way he had come up. He had stood too long there on the crest of the ridge. The sun was already half swallowed by the night, and the shadows were dark and tall in the bowl of the valley under the trees. It would be sleeping time before he reached the campfire. Yovo would be worried. Kontu wondered why the priest did not go himself each evening to see how the land lay ahead of them.

He knew the answer. Yovo was old, Kontu was young. Yovo was a priest with great responsibilities. Kontu was learning to be a priest and learning to take on responsibilities. Yovo meant for it to weigh heavily upon him that he was the one whose duty it was every day to stare between the south and the setting sun for a path or a gap or a landmark.

For all that Kontu had seen, it might as well have been the dim eyes of Yovo spying out their route. And every time he had taken too long on the errand and been scolded by the priest. "There are Primitives in these woods," the old man would say with a rough shake of the shoulders. "Don't be so foolish. They can see in the dark, and a lone man in the trees after sunset is just what they like to meet."

Kontu hurried now, looking quickly about him at the thick shadows under the rocks. Everyone knew that Primitives lived in this part of the country; the little squat men who had only their spears for weapons, using no throwing stick to hurl them; who made no pottery or baskets, using only shells and bark for containers. Strong and fearless little men who hated the Adena people and were in turn hated. What would they do to him, if they caught him? Fear prickled down his neck.

He was glad to see the campfire among the trees. He slowed his steps. No point in showing his fright to the others. Likely there were no Primitives among these ridges where game was scarce. Certainly, so far there had been no sign of them.

Kontu braced himself. Yovo was staring among the trees, waiting for a first glimpse of him. "Ah, at last," cried the old priest. "What have you been up to? You have been gone too long. What did you see?"

"I saw no path," answered Kontu. "Trees and more trees, and another ridge lies ahead of us."

"Well, then what took you so long?" raged Yovo. Kontu was ashamed. The old man really worried about him. He should make an effort always to be back at camp before dark. "I was waiting," he said at last. "Waiting to see something, a sign, anything." It was true. Every twilight he expected to see some wonder ahead, something to assure him that their mission was not in vain.

Yovo was scornful. "A sign? Without prayers, without song, without fasting?" he cried. "Your head is as hard as a ball of flint! Come eat."

But signs were sometimes given without fasting and dancing and rituals. Kontu knew it and so did Yovo. Out of nowhere there would come a flash of power, a shining token, and everyone would know what to do. It might happen any time, any place, to any person.

The food was snake. Gunt had killed two snakes by a spring, and now the four of them were provided with a meal. They had not eaten too well of late. Yovo liked them to stay close together, and it did not make finding or killing game very easy, four travelers trotting through the woods on each other's heels. They ate what they could get and sometimes that was very little.

And in truth Gunt was a poor hunter anyway. Kontu was surprised that he had been able to kill even slow-moving snakes, for he was awkward and thick-headed, not good with any weapon, not really good at anything, ball-playing or running or singing or fire-making. Kontu had been surprised when Gunt had said he would go with them, even more surprised when Yovo had agreed to his coming.

But then, of course, it must be pleasant for Gunt to be away from the village where even children jeered at him for his clumsiness. Kontu had noticed a long time back that Gunt often spent days in the forest for no reason except to be alone. It was a strange way for an Adena warrior, nearly as old as Kontu's own father, to act.

When they had eaten, Gunt rolled over and went to sleep. Watota, on the contrary, began a long story about how he had once hunted a bear. He was only a few years older than Kontu, and as an unproven warrior he was eager to make himself seem grown-up and a fierce hunter, and he told such stories every night.

Kontu was often bored with these tales, which went on and on, about the length of the bear's claws and teeth, about the thickness of its fur and the terribleness of its roar, and about how swiftly and cleverly Watota could fit the butt of his spear into the notch of his throwing stick to make the weapon travel farther and with more power.

Yovo listened with great attentiveness, nodding his head often to show that he was paying close heed, clicking his tongue to show that he was impressed with Watota's strength and prowess. Nevertheless, Kontu thought the old priest never really thought about the bear's teeth and Watota's courage, or anything except their mission. When the story ended Yovo always hastened to say the same thing. "Tomorrow we must hurry on our way again. Tomorrow we must retrace the path that the Adena people followed through the forest when the Sacred Eagle led them away from the sleeping Eye, led them beyond the Crystal River to new homes. We must be up early tomorrow. The Eye awaits our coming. No more time for talk. Time for sleep."

Time for sleep, Kontu agreed. He was bone-weary, for Yovo drove them hard and kept them walking all day at a good pace. The grass and moss were soft under his out-stretched body, the fire blazed and its warmth covered him. He was asleep before the star he watched through a hole in the branches over him had traveled a finger's breadth across the sky.

When he awoke, he felt the cold. Some creature cried mournfully far off in the night. The fire was very low and would be dead before morning if he didn't throw a few sticks on it. He reached out and then stopped. What was that? Did something, someone move, just outside the circle of dim light? Was that a stooped stocky figure there by Watota and another by the priest? And did a third small man bend over the priest's sacred bundle, ready to draw out the sacred things which must not be touched by any defiled hand?

Kontu lay frozen, unable to move. If the creatures were real, he was afraid. If they were dreams or ghosts or witches, he was more afraid still. He wanted to call out, but could find no voice.

But suddenly his muscles moved; he jumped for the pile of wood near him and tossed a handful on the ashes. The wood was dry and seasoned, sparks flew up and the fire blazed in a dazzling upward flight. Kontu stared around, feeling for his flint knife and ax. There was no one to be seen anywhere except the four travelers. No dwarfish in-truders lurked and the Sacred Packet was untouched.

He added more wood to the fire and lay back down. Had it been a dream then? Or had the little men scurried into the darkness in those first moments when he was blinded by the spurt of flames? Surely if those men had been real, the four Adena would be dead now. Primitives were not known for mercy. And the sacred things would now be scattered about the woods, for what good would they be to those with no beliefs?

It had to be a dream. A good dream or a bad dream? Should he tell Yovo and perhaps have him turn back home? Who knew what to do? He closed his eyes and fell once more far far into sleep.

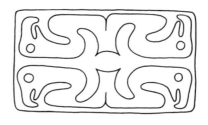

Chapter Two

Yovo woke Kontu, shaking him roughly. "Get up, get up," cried the old man sharply. "You sleep till sunup every morning. It's not the way. A priest must be up by first birdcall."

Kontu was confused and even a little frightened. He couldn't at first remember where he was, or why he was there. He had been so deeply asleep. Now he saw that the sky was beginning to lighten, and he remembered his dream, and he sprang up. He must tell Yovo. But the old priest had turned away, fussing at the others to get their things together at once. Kontu said nothing, seeing that it would be better to wait till the morning ritual was over and Yovo had time to listen.

He walked naked through the gray woods to the spring. In its cold water he washed, and as the water flowed over him he asked it to carry away to some far place all the evil that he had touched since last he bathed. Standing, he looked up through the dark leafy boughs to the saffron sky. Then he said his prayers to the great soaring Eagle, Life, and to Tobacco, the Sacred Breath, and to Fire, without whom Tobacco was useless.

Back at the campfire he dressed, pulling his breechcloth of elkskin through his legs and fastening it around his waist with a belt. He fixed his flint knife and stone ax at his side. He had no weighted throwing stick nor spear, as the two warriors did. He could use these things, but not well. A priest had no time nor need for practicing the art of slaughter. Kontu had been given to the priesthood when he was very small. Ever since, his time had been spent in learning to prolong Adena life, to propitiate the spirit world, and hours on hours in gathering herbs and practicing chants, in prayer and more prayer. Some things a boy had to give up.

Kontu wondered. He would have made a better hunter and warrior than Gunt, he felt sure. Who knew what kind of priest he would be? It worried him that perhaps he should not have been taken by the priest cult as an initiate. Sometimes he thought he would never learn all there was to know. Perhaps he should have spent those hours practicing with a spear rather than learning the way to call forth the Snake Spirit.

"Hurry, Kontu, hurry!" cried Yovo, and Watota, who was all ready to leave, grinned a little. He always seemed to like to hear Yovo scold Kontu.

"I'm ready," said Kontu coldly and he stared hard at Watota.

"You have not eaten," Yovo reminded him.

"I can eat as we go," Kontu assured him. Gunt would give him dried deermeat from his pack, Kontu knew. It was supposed to be eaten only if there was an emergency, and looking around at their camp, Kontu saw that the emergency had come. The others had left him nothing.

The old man sighed impatiently. But he prepared to leave. He put his hand on his medicine bag sewn to the breast of his shirt. The bag was made of a part of a rattlesnake's skin with the rattles still attached. He rubbed his fingers over the mottled skin as if to draw strength from his medicine inside, as if to find courage for the coming day's ordeal.

Suddenly, the strands of grass holding the bag to his shirt broke under his hand, and the bag slipped away and fell to the ground and split open. The things inside spilled over the moss. The other three turned away at once. It would never do to look at those holy objects, even though they had fallen to the earth and lay for anyone to see.

But Kontu wished he had had a glimpse of them; he longed to know what the priest kept in the little snakeskin sack. Someday he would have such a small pack himself, magic things to help him, personal relics of dreams and good happenings and lucky omens, and his bag might be made of a toad's skin, or some other animal's. He did not know what his medicine would be, for it lay in the future, but he was filled with curiosity about it nevertheless.

The three stood waiting, and at last Yovo spoke. His voice was full of apprehension. "We will not be able to travel today," he said. He seemed almost fearful of speaking. "This is a bad thing that has happened. Something dangerous is in the air. We will have to discover what it is."

Kontu remembered his dream. He should have told Yovo at once. Now perhaps he had caused this very bad thing to happen by not telling what he had seen or dreamed.

Gunt said, "If there is danger about, maybe we should go on. No point in waiting for Primitives to attack, or bears, or whatever the bad thing is. I think perhaps we ought to go on."

Yovo glanced at him scornfully. "I do not think it is Primitives or bears we have to fear," he answered calmly enough. "It is bad magic, some kind of wickedness that threatens our magic. We *cannot* escape it by going on. No, we must take the time to discover what the wickedness is or else we are in greater danger by going on than by staying here."

Gunt shrugged and turned away. It was no concern of his or Watota's. It was a thing for priests. Watota let his pack slip to the ground and sat down with his back against a tree and began to inspect his spear, going over the blade's bindings carefully and feeling the flint's edge with his thumb.

Kontu envied him a little. Probably Gunt and Watota both would leave in a while and go hunting or fishing; it was all they were asked to do. But he, Kontu, now would have to tell Yovo about his dream and the priest would be angry, in all likelihood, and blame him for the way the medicine bag had broken. The priest would scold him for being too stupid to know what was a sign and what was not. And there would be the long ceremony and prayers to set matters right again. In this the warriors would have no part, whereas Kontu would spend hours chanting and fetching dried herbs and blowing on the small holy fire.

With a sigh he looked up, for now was the time to face Yovo. He wished the others would go away and not listen to his story. But they did not go. There was no help for it; he had to speak out.

Yovo frowned as he listened. "You should have mentioned this as soon as you awoke," he snapped. "Then this other misfortune might have been avoided." He looked really worried. Kontu was remorseful. He should have been a warrior, not a priest.

Yovo picked up his pack with the sacred objects. Chanting softly to himself, he walked slowly off among the trees and Kontu followed. They did not go far. When Yovo reached a place where the sun slanted between two tall trees, he stopped and knelt and put the pack on the ground.

He went on chanting as he worked at laying out the paraphernalia and making the holy fire.

Kontu joined in the chanting, but Yovo shook his head at him and he stoppped. Yovo did not even ask him to fetch wood for the fire, but he himself went and cut the green twigs and gathered the dry bark for the flames and threw on the magic powders that made the fire burn low and turn red and then blue. Finally, he added a pinch of this herb and that herb and the morning air was filled with their acrid scent.

Suddenly, Yovo stood up and seized the boy by his shoulders and pressed him to his knees. Kontu was frightened. Perhaps Yovo was going to break in his skull for having done this stupid thing. Kontu had heard of such killings being done by priests. It was better to destroy a young man who had learned magic and its secret ways but not learned how to use such power properly. But Yovo had no weapon, he did not look fierce.

Now Yovo chanted louder and began to dance around the fire, in and out of the purifying smoke till it swirled and swayed with his body. Pulling Kontu backward onto the earth, he arranged his arms and legs so that he lay like two crossed sticks, pointing four ways at once to the four quarters of the earth circle. Yovo stroked him along his limbs with an eagle feather to wipe away unseen hands. Streamers of smoke curled about them. The chanting grew louder.

In place of the feather a small gourd appeared in the priest's hand. He dipped from it a strange-smelling oil and rubbed it on a spot in the center of his forehead and then on a spot in the center of Kontu's forehead. The boy knew now that he was being prepared for a trance, that Yovo wanted him to go back into his dream of last night and discover more about what it meant. He was excited and his heart pounded; the light shimmered before his eyes as it fell through the trees. It was his first real priestly experience and his first real magic. The smells of oil and herbs and fire swirled around him and he felt strange, as though his head had swelled up bigger than his whole body.

Yovo leaned over and rubbed the boy's lips with a bitter substance. The world grew darker and darker while at the same time the fire spread over him brighter and brighter; the voices of flowers sang in his ears and under him the earth turned and twisted until it shook Kontu loose and he felt himself rise from the ground and float—lying on the air as a leaf lies on the water. All around him, blue light thundered and red light screamed.

Kontu was afraid; creatures without faces peered at him out of the light and eyes without bodies stared at him from the dark and thick flames reached out for him from every direction. He shrieked and fell, falling and falling, and then suddenly he was standing on the firm earth. He no longer felt strange except that his body had no weight and it seemed he might float off into the skies, the very air he breathed seemed to leak out through the pores of his skin.

It was delight. He had never been so happy, so peaceful, so sure of himself. All around him grew trees, taller and stronger and straighter than any trees he had ever seen, and under his feet grew flowers and grasses of many colors. It was beautiful. Before him up a hillside the great trees grew one after another, up a slope so steep it seemed a man could not climb it. Yet the trees grew in pride and in vigor, all up that cliffside.

Kontu walked along the bottom of it and came at last to a little rushing, roaring river, falling from level to level in one white-foamed cataract after another. But search as he might there was no way to the top, no path through that tower of forest marching up the hill. Kontu turned around and walked the other way among the great trees and with the tall wall of the hill looming over him. On he walked till he came to another river, like the first one, a series of foaming pools and swift falls.

But here he found a sort of path that wound up among the rocks and he went up it, slowly, for it was not an easy path to follow. It lost itself among the boulders, and he had to retrace his steps twice. At last he came to the top, to a kind of earthen wall along the top of the wooded slope and inside the wall a smooth green meadow, without a sign of human habitation, without a grazing deer or trotting fox or even a woodchuck sunning on the grasses. Only the wind moved over that brilliant green field, gently, gently through the sunlight.

It was the Eye in the Forest, Kontu knew. This was the place where his ancestors had lived and had kept sacred the earth and the sky and the green of life. And in return they had been given goodness and protection from evil. He stood there in awe of the place and its holiness and its great age, till at last he felt himself drawn by the Eye's force across the open meadow. And there in the very center was the pupil of the Eye, a clear spring bubbling up and forming a small deep pool reflecting the sky and nothing more, bright and mysterious and alive.

Kontu cried aloud. It was almost more than he could bear, to be in so beautiful and sacred a place, to be here where all things were purified and without shame or stain.

Suddenly the sky darkened. He glanced up and there was no cloud—only the sky seemed to have lowered toward the earth and its color was no longer blue and fadeless, but a strange yellow-gray color in which the sun was entangled, dim and troubled. The air was no longer cool and fresh, but full of something bad, something stale and stinking.

His sweet strange feeling of weightlessness was gone, lost, and he seemed now to be heavier than if he had a stone on his head. His breath came grittily in and out of his lungs. The grass under his feet was coarse and dry, scarcely green at all. The little pond was dank and covered with scum; and the trees—the great marvelous trees—oh, what had happened? These scrawny broken things, scarcely able to hold up their warped and diseased branches, they could not be the same trees, could not be!

But what terrified him most were the ugly things scattered about the field and down the slope, the things made out of materials he did not know of, cold and harsh to the hand, rough and broken and red with some kind of ruinous fungus, hideous things, broken and useless, left there to die, but still alive and full of pain and evil. What repulsive shapes the things were, lying about smothering the grass, menacing even the vines that struggled to cover them.

What dreadful thing had befallen the Eye in the Forest in that moment, what curse had been put on it and on him, so that he could not breathe, could not stand, could not live! He screamed and screamed and screamed and someone said, "Hush, hush!" And Kontu opened his eyes and thought he must still be dreaming.

For he lay in the woods beside the holy fire and Yovo sat next to him and there beyond were Gunt and Watota, weaponless and bound, and all around them the little squat dark men he had seen the night before.

The Primitives!

Chapter Three

Kontu raised himself dizzily on his elbows, but Yovo shoved him back to the ground. "Lie still," the priest said. "Don't speak!" his eyes commanded.

Kontu lay silent staring up at the sky, feeling frightened of the dream that had possessed him and frightened of what was happening here in the world of real things and people. Or perhaps it was not the world of real things and people. He struggled again to sit up but Yovo held him firmly and then began to rub oil into the boy's forehead.

Then it *was* real. The smell of the burning herbs was too sharp and pungent, the touch of Yovo's rough hands too warm and urgent to be things in a dream. And the Primitives—a ring of ugliness and menacing spears around—real, too real!

After a while Yovo pulled Kontu to his feet and led him to the fire. The priest threw something on the flames and a long spurt of blue flame shot up around the two of them. The Primitives gasped and shifted back uneasily. Yovo cried out in a strong voice of thanksgiving to the spirit world for the safe return of Kontu.

The ceremony was done; Yovo asked, "Are you all right?" and Kontu nodded. He felt strange and confused but no longer weak and dizzy. He stood looking around. Watota and Gunt sat indifferently, trying to look as though getting captured by these small gnomes was nothing more than getting caught in a rainstorm, just a happening that would soon be over.

As for the Primitives, they stood well back from the embers of the Sacred Fire and the priest and his pupil. Yovo's magic was terrible to them and threatening and dangerous, Kontu could tell. He was suddenly very proud of the old man and even of his own small knowledge of sacred matters. How much wiser they were than these little men who probably knew no more of such things than did the leaves of the trees.

At last one of the Primitives stepped closer. He had queer markings on his cheeks and chin and must be the leader, Kontu thought. With gestures and a few words in a language Yovo seemed to partly understand, he made it plain that the captives were to come with them. Kontu was certain the old man would protest, but instead he set the boy to work packing the sacred objects. Then they shouldered their bundles and started off in the midst of the Primitives. Suddenly, the priest halted and a great cry came thundering from him.

Kontu was startled, but the Primitives leaped back among the trees. Yovo pointed his finger at the leader and grunted an angry word or two, then turned and pointed at Watota and Gunt, still tied to trees and guarded by a few of the little men.

The leader shook his head. With gestures Yovo seemed to ask a question, and with gestures and head shakes the leader answered.

Yovo turned and stepped quickly to the two warriors. Drawing his knife, he slashed their bonds. The leader of the Primitives uttered a quick word to his followers and motioned them back as they came forward in protest.

"Stay here," Yovo said to the warriors, "for the Primitives do not want you in their village. I do not know

why—with Primitives there is no reason for doing things."
He sheathed the knife.

"There is something wrong in their village. That much I can understand from their leader. And he believes Kontu and I can right that wrong because we are priests. We will go but we will return here." He moved away, then stopped and added, "But do not leave this place or we will not be able to find you. You are safe till we return."

The Primitive leader called out to the guards and they sat down holding their spears, alert, close to the two Adena warriors. Kontu glanced back to see Gunt and Watota rubbing life back into their hands and arms and staring after the others.

The little men do not need that many guards for *those* two, he thought and then was ashamed. Who was he to criticize the others when he could scarcely throw a spear himself or fight with an ax as Gunt could?

Yovo looked back once also, and then he said to the boy walking behind him, "You are thinking I did wrong to leave them." He paused and Kontu made no reply, though he was indeed thinking just that. "I had no choice, though the Primitives are frightened of my power. If I had refused to go, they would have selected one of them to kill us all, then that one would have to leave the group. Evil would lie on him for our deaths; so by going away, he would take the evil away and the rest would be safe."

Kontu nodded though he was scarcely listening to the words. He was too frightened. And Yovo was scared too. Kontu could tell the old man was being pushed to the limits of his strength. A ritual of magic such as he had already performed this morning was wearying to a priest. And now this. The old sorcerer might collapse. Then what would happen to the three Adena?

There was small doubt about that. The priest was their sacred talisman, their only hope to live.

The path they traveled was not the one Yovo would have had them take this morning. It angled up a slope, steep and difficult to follow. Yovo stumbled and fell more than once. At last they reached the ridgetop, but they did not stop. The Primitive leader hurried them on. Kontu had a quick look and saw there was much open land below and scattered groves of trees.

The path plunged down the other side between huge rocks. They came to the edge of a cliff where a waterfall dropped straight to the bottom of the ridge. There had been high water lately. At the very edge of the drop a log was jammed and debris piled behind it. Kontu was surprised to find himself wondering how much longer the rotting log would hold.

They climbed slowly down beside the falls, stepping from one slippery rock to another, spray blowing over them. Kontu stayed close to Yovo, but the old man eased carefully over the wet rocks without a mishap. Now the path wound through a pine woods to the bottom of the ridge. Here the way was wide and well-worn, tall ferns hid the stream that ran beside it.

The trees were thin and Kontu could catch glimpses of a camp and a few people. High overhead vultures circled, many of them. As always the sight of them clutched at Kontu's innards. He never liked to see them tilting in the bright air.

They were good omens, cleansing birds, Yovo said. But Kontu could not forget that last year when his uncle went into the hills to fast and pray and did not return, it was the vultures hovering over his body at the foot of a cliff which had guided the searchers to him. Vultures meant death.

Yovo glanced up too; Kontu saw the old man's face tighten. It was fear that made the skin grow tense around his mouth. "What is it?" the boy asked.

"Hush," said Yovo. "We will soon know."

A few yards farther along, they came on a great crowd of the black carrion eaters on the ground tearing at something. Kontu stared. It was a human body. He was shocked that the Primitives cared so little for their dead ones as to leave them lying where they fell. The birds flapped off silently, but they settled back as soon as the men passed. There was a stench of rotting flesh in the air.

The village was only a scatter of shelters among the trees at the edge of the grasslands, mostly frames covered with cane or leafy branches. Scarcely protection from the sun's heat, much less rain or wind or cold. But then the Primitives were hunters, moving after herds of deer and elk, and they would hardly waste time building houses as secure and tidy as those the Adena built.

Their hunts had evidently been successful of late, for skins of these beasts were spread across bushes to dry, antlers and bones lay in heaps among the shelters. Men and women and a child or two sat among the huts or leaned against trees or stumps. They did not come to greet the returning party; they only stared, looking stunned and blank, as though somehow their souls had left them and only bodies remained to crouch in the dust. Only when they saw Kontu and Yovo drawing near did a few of them get up and slip away, looking fearful.

Ahead was a kind of house, at least it had walls of skins and bark and bundles of cane. It stood away from the others, and their guide led them toward it. The other Primitives turned aside one by one till, when they reached the house, there was only the small leader, the old priest, and his young initiate. Kontu was afraid. What was inside the rough dwelling? What had happened at this camp? Why did the Primitives think the two of them could help? And what was going to happen to them if they could do nothing?

At last the leader halted. He turned his head listening. From the hut came strange bubbling noises and heavy choked breathing. The little Primitive pointed with his spear, swept them toward the door with a wide gesture of his arm.

Yovo shook his head. He eased the pack from his back and nodded at it and spoke a few words. The leader glared and then reluctantly nodded and walked off to one side. He sat down under a tree with two of the men who had been in his party.

"What is it they want?" Kontu whispered. "Why are we here?"

"A bad thing has happened. An evil has come upon these people. And the Primitives do not know much holiness," answered Yovo. "That is why we are here."

He began to lay out the sacred articles they would need. The antler headdress of copper, for copper had a strange hard softness that was respected by people and spirits alike and so had power always. The rattles, the bowl of sacred fire that was never allowed to go out, and a few bags of herbs Yovo arranged in careful rows.

Yovo began attaching the copper antlers to his head. He glanced around and the Primitives watching turned their eyes and looked away. "Now quickly, tell me . . . if you dreamed . . . if you had a sign. . . . I must know." He picked up the rattles to strap on his legs.

So Kontu told the dream. He did not want to tell the last part. It seemed so dreadful a thing and anyway he did not know how to describe it, did not know how to make Yovo see a world worn thin and grimy and juiceless, yet still full of harsh and hideous things. But he knew he must tell it all and did his best. Yovo listened attentively. His expression was the same as when he was listening to Watota tell how he killed the bear. He said nothing, but nodded often.

· 21 ·

When the boy had finished, the priest muttered softly, "The Eye is there. Yes, it waits. And it knows where its scattered people are. It calls on them. It will draw us to it. Perhaps in time to prevent this evil of your vision."

He strapped a terrapin shell filled with pebbles to his arms. Then he looked at Kontu, and the boy saw something deep in his eyes that he did not like. "Perhaps that is what your dream means. Though now I'm too weary to probe its depths."

He took the cover from the sacred pot of fire which they had brought from the temple of their village. He blew on it and added fine powdery wood and small twigs from the ground. "Take this carefully before you," he told Kontu. "Now we are ready. Our fate depends on Fire and Tobacco and Snake." He fingered the snakeskin medicine bag at his chest. "Snake hides and listens and glides unseen everywhere. He will know what evil lies here and will help us."

He stood and drew a deep breath into his chest. "They must help us if help is to come at all," he went on. "Kontu, you and I have come to the edge of living!"

He began to chant. His voice was not old Father Yovo's voice, but the loud cold hollow echo of Yovo's voice, as it always was at these times. Kontu joined in the prayer to Snake for help and safety. "Oh, Snake! Snake!" prayed Kontu. "Protect us, help us!" He lifted his eyes and saw suddenly the house of skins, where something monstrous lay, where he and Yovo must go. His prayers suddenly stopped as the priest's words roared through his head—the edge of living!

Chapter Four

Yovo moved toward the doorway of the hut. He moved as priests knew how, as Kontu was learning how, so that the rattles tied to his arms and legs shook and made a great deal of noise, yet Yovo did not appear to be causing them to shake. The priest pushed through the flap of skin over the doorway and entered.

Kontu knew he should follow at once with the Sacred Fire. Still he hesitated for a second and glanced around at the Primitives gathered to watch. The warriors gripped their spears grimly. Then he too pushed past the skin door, carefully, so that nothing touched his bowl of fire.

It was very dark. There was no fire on the hearth, and only a little light came through the smokehole in the roof and a dull glow from Kontu's bowl. It was fearfully hot in there, however, and a heavy fetid smell of evil and illness made it seem even hotter. The evil did more than smell, it reached out and touched; Kontu could feel it crawl along his skin.

Yovo chanted and chanted, his voice louder and louder in order that the evil spirits might know how powerful a one came here, ready to pit himself against them. He danced the rattles about the dwelling, moving slowly and cautiously through the dark, and he continued to sing.

Kontu held his bowl and followed as best he could. He chanted too, over and over, the sacred words that implored help from Snake and Fire.

Suddenly, something grabbed Kontu's leg and dug sharp nails into his flesh. He gave a frightened cry and tried to jerk away, and the embers fell from the bowl to the floor and lay glowing in the dust beside a death's-head of skin and bones and wild leaping eyes. The man clutched the boy's leg harder in an effort to raise himself but he was too weak and fell back twisting and contorting and clawing. Froth bubbled out between his cracked lips and he snarled and shrieked.

Kontu was scared almost beyond endurance, but he fought to steady himself. Then he swiftly knelt and picked up the coals with his bare fingers. He blistered his fingertips, but he could not care and forced himself to pick up every bit of the Fire. He was responsible for the Fire; how could he have done such a thing as to let it fall to the earth in this evil place? It was even worse that he had been scared and dropped it. A priest never let fear possess him, nor did one training to be a priest.

Yovo continued to dance and sing, praying and praying that he might prevail against the horrible devils in this dark place. Kontu hoped the priest had not seen the Sacred Fire spill to the floor, but the chanting went on so long Kontu believed he must have, that the priest had had to pray longer and harder to make up for this wrongdoing. Though his legs had turned to useless strings and his voice was no more than a weak croak, Kontu danced and sang on behind the priest. How could the old man keep on?

Finally Yovo whirled faster and faster around the man on the floor, and his song boomed through the hut like summer thunder and with one last Hu! Ya! Ho! the priest stopped. He had been successful. The chief lay still, his limbs relaxed, his breathing, though harsh and loud, was even and quick.

For a moment Kontu thought Yovo was going to fall to the floor beside the man, the old priest looked so tired and spent. Then with a deep breath Yovo threw back his head and straightened up. He took the bowl of Fire from the boy and went to the hearth and, using some sticks and moss laid to one side, built a fire kindled from the Sacred Bowl.

The light blazed up; Kontu could see all the inside of the hut, dirty and untidy, not neatly swept and clean like the house of an Adena leader, but cluttered and in disarray. He could see where the man had left his bed and crawled about in the dust. Perhaps his pain had been so terrible he could not lie still, but had wandered about knocking over weapons and scattering skins.

Yovo sat down by the fire. He looked so old and tired, Kontu was amazed. How had such a broken thin stick of a man done such a thing, captured the evil that was living here and bound it so that it no longer roamed free and full of power? He felt enormously proud of his teacher-father.

Yovo took some leaves from his magic purse and sitting there by the flames, chewed them slowly. Then he threw two or three of the leaves on the fire and watched them burn. He drew up his knees, crossed his arms on top of them, and rested his head on his arms. At once he was asleep.

Kontu sat, feeding moss and twigs to the fire to keep it blazing, listening to the hard sound of the sick man's breathing, and listening for any sound from outside, for the approach of the men with spears and knives and the women with clubs to kill him little by little. After a bit, he too relaxed. He did not sleep, but he no longer listened and he no longer feared. What would happen would happen and he must trust Fire and Snake and Tobacco to see that somehow they would survive this ordeal, and Yovo would find the Eye and save the Adena people.

He wondered if the Primitives had an Eye somewhere that might have protected them from whatever this horror was which had fallen upon them. But no, they knew so little of medicine and magic, nothing like the Sacred Eye in the Forest would ever have been bestowed upon them. The proof was that although so many bad things had happened to the Adena, although they were indeed in danger, and although hunger and sickness had come among them, there had never been anything so terrible and full of wickedness as what was here in this strange little encampment, in this dark hut.

Yovo stirred and lifted his head. It had not been a long time he slept but he looked much refreshed and rested. Kontu's heart lifted. The old man's powers were beyond belief. He would see that they came to no harm.

"Move the man back to his bed," he ordered.

Kontu rose to do as he was told. The Primitive was so wasted away from his illness that the boy stretched him out on his skin pallet with ease. The man screamed and his hands clawed at his legs, but he did not open his eyes.

"Now fetch my pack and yours," the priest said.

Fear gripped Kontu again, he did not want to go alone out of the hut and face the Primitives. But he had been commanded to do it, and he did. Outside, he forced himself to meet the stony glances of the groups of little men and women, but he dropped his eyes almost at once. If evil spirits possessed all these people, then it was best not to look at them too carefully. When he picked up the bundles his blistered fingers burned and stung, but he did not care. He had retrieved the Sacred Fire in spite of great pain, and Fire would perhaps forgive him because of that.

In the hut he handed Yovo the packs. He whispered,

"They are waiting outside with their weapons. They have come close to the hut. They are ready to kill us."

"Hush!" said Yovo fiercely. "Begin the prayer for health, the one that speaks to the bird which flies higher than the cloud. . . ."

Kontu concentrated. He would remember the prayer exactly, he would make no error, no little slip where the wicked spirits could get back their power and fatten their evil on the Primitives.

He chanted; Yovo chanted. In a bowl the old man mixed herbs and a little liquid from a gourd and stirred and stirred. He took from among his gear a sort of comb with teeth made of the fangs of snakes. Still chanting, he moved to kneel beside the sick man and began to run this comb along the patient's arms and legs. Red welts followed the teeth of the comb, blood oozed from them. Once or twice the man groaned and stirred a bit.

When Yovo had scratched the man's arms and legs, he scratched his chest and thighs. Kontu thought now surely the last of the evil would be gone, for the ceremony was to aid the herbal medicine to get inside the sick person. Yovo laid aside the comb and then began to rub an ointment into the wounds, singing softly all the while, a different chant now; but Kontu still sang over and over the cry for help to the swift, the small black bird with no feet that flew forever above the clouds. When it was done, the priest and his helper crouched by the bed, and there was only a very soft sound of rattles going on and on and the crackle of the blaze on the hearth.

Then suddenly, the chieftain sighed and opened his eyes. He looked at them curiously but without fright. The sickness was almost gone from his face. Kontu was amazed at the way he looked, like a man who has been ill but is now a long way toward getting well.

The patient spoke weakly, but the words made no sense to either of them. Yovo rose and went to the door of the hut. Kontu saw him beckon and heard him call out. After a moment the Primitive who had led the band of their captors came into the house.

When he saw his chieftain, his face lit up and he smiled and spoke. For a while the two Primitives, the chief and the warrior, talked together. Then the warrior turned to Yovo and tried to tell him something, but Yovo could not understand. At last the leader said something sharply to the warrior and turned his head away and shut his eyes, as though the effort was too much for him.

Kontu quaked. Was the man going to die anyway, right there before their eyes? The warrior made a shrugging motion with his shoulders and went out. Yovo picked up his bowl of liquid and, raising the sick man's head, forced him to drink—three long swallows. When the man lay back on his skins, Yovo turned to Kontu and spoke quietly.

"The other has gone to get a third person, one who speaks the tongue of the Adena, if the few words I understood are right," he said. "I knew there must be such a one in the camp, it is almost always true. We are a great and important people, and nearly everywhere there is some person who can understand our language well enough."

Yovo edged closer to the boy. "Now listen carefully," he continued, "for I will not be able to speak to you after this person is present. We are in greater danger than you know, for the man will die. I have seen this evil spirit before and often it behaves like this. When a powerful magic comes against it, it is afraid and hides in the ear. It makes itself very small and hides very well and the magic often cannot find it, no matter how powerful."

He paused to listen. There was only a murmur of talk among the watchers outside, no hurrying footsteps. "But then after a few hours the evil darts from the ear inside the man's head, runs right behind his eyes, so that he screams, he twists . . . then blood pours from his ears and nose, his eyes start from his head, and in an instant he is dead. That is what will happen to this one here, I am nearly certain."

He gestured toward the bed. "We must make certain that we are well away before it happens to him. So be prepared. And whatever I say to do, do at once."

Kontu nodded, staring at the doomed man. He was glad the evil was frightened now and had hidden away, but he did not like the thought that it was still here in the hut with them.

The skin door was pushed aside. The Primitive warrior entered once again, dragging along with him a girl, not much older than Kontu. She was not a Primitive, neither was she one of the Adena. The warrior shoved her roughly toward the bed, and she snarled a string of words at him. She looked wild and strange to Kontu, but she spoke directly and without fear.

"I speak the language of the Adena people," she said at once to Yovo. "Speak slowly and I can understand you and interpret."

"Yes," nodded Yovo. "It is good. We have done what was asked of us and cured this chieftain. Now we must leave. We have imprisoned the evil and we will leave behind us a magic to keep it imprisoned. Tell him this and that now we leave. And if he tries to keep us, I will let the evil out and give it something strong to make it grow."

The girl grinned sourly. "I will tell what you said," she nodded to Yovo. "But if they let you leave, where will you go, old man?"

"Why should I tell you?" the priest asked. "So if the chief dies, you might tell the Primitives where to look for us?"

Again the girl smiled her smile that had no gaiety or light in it. "I hate these little dwarfs of men," she answered. "I have been a slave among them more than six moons. I would never betray another to them. No, I thought I might mislead them if it happened the chieftain dies very soon. For he will die, I think. But I would not tell where you had gone."

"Then a blessing on you, Daughter," replied Yovo. "But they know we have to go back by the waterfall path to our friends who are being held. We are on our way far to the south . . . on a great mission."

The girl frowned. "I will do what I can for you," she said. "And I will tell you that fire awes these people more than any other thing. It is a thing to remember."

"Fire is powerful," agreed Yovo. And he took off the copper antlers and began to gather the sacred things as the girl talked to the chief. Kontu kept his eyes on the sick man, who spoke quickly to the warrior. The chieftain was afraid, Kontu could tell, though he did not know of what. The warrior shook his head, and the two Primitives talked back and forth for some moments.

At last the girl turned back to Yovo. "The chief wants to let you go. He does not like having magicians in his town. He feels well and is hungry," she said. "But the warrior wants to see your magic and judge how powerful it is before letting you leave."

The priest nodded and took two eagle feathers from his pack. Kontu was surprised, for these feathers were sacred and valuable. Yovo chanted and drew the feathers slowly through the flames on the hearth. They did not singe nor burn and the warrior gasped. Then the old man laid the feathers crosswise on one of the stones of the hearth. "Tell them the evil is held here under this stone and the feathers will guard it and keep it there," he told the girl. "Tell them if they try to prevent us from leaving, the feathers will fly away."

After the girl had repeated his words, Yovo flung a handful of powder on the fire and green and red flames shot up with a sudden howling sound that rose up through the smokehole to hover and wail itself out high above the hut. Startled, the chief sat up in bed and the warrior fled through the doorway.

"You are very clever, old man," the girl exclaimed. "May the snakes not sting you, nor the thorns cut your flesh on your journey."

Yovo smiled at her with kindness. Kontu knew that he was pleased that the girl had remembered the Adena farewell to travelers. The priest slipped the straps of the sacred bundle over his shoulders. To the girl he said, "Keep yourself in courage, Daughter, the Sacred Eye watches over you." To Kontu he said, "We go, but very slowly and with dignity."

Kontu picked up the bowl of Fire and covered it and placed it in its supports on Yovo's pack. With not so much as a glance at the chief nor one word, Yovo walked toward the door, putting one foot carefully in front of the other. Kontu followed with his pack, almost stepping on the old man's heels in his anxiety to leave the hut. Out of the corner of his eyes, he saw the look of relief on the chief's face. Priests and their magic made him uneasy and he was glad to be rid of them, in spite of their help.

They passed outside to find the Primitives scattering before them in panic. They moved through the camp in their slow solemn walk, looking straight ahead. Kontu was sure he could not keep this pace much longer. At his back he could feel the chieftain's life coming and going in little breaths, and who knew which would be his last? They walked and walked and at last they were invisible, the forest and the curves of the path hid them from the camp. Now they hurried. But the way up the ridge zigzagged through woods and was steep and shadowy, Yovo could not go very fast. Kontu was frightened, he kept glancing over his shoulder; he pushed ahead of Yovo and then waited for the old man. He could hear the waterfall roar in front of them. Yovo would have trouble on those slippery rocks.

They climbed on. At last the old man gasped, "I must rest." He was gray-faced with weariness. He sat down and closed his eyes, and Kontu looked down at his tired and wrinkled face. Yovo sat thus for a long time and Kontu's heart thudded with fear.

And then he heard what he had dreaded to hear—faint sounds of cries and wild shouts. The chieftain was dead then, and the Primitives knew they had been tricked, and they would come to avenge themselves on the priest and his helper.

"Listen, Father Yovo," he cried. "The Primitives are coming!" He pulled the old man to his feet. "We must hurry." But where and why, he did not know. How could they hope to escape those little hunters who must know this country as well as the deer who roamed the hills and woods?

The old man stood, looking dazed and unsteady on his feet. Kontu knew suddenly that he was the one who must save them now. He grasped the priest by his shoulders and pushed him ahead of him. "Hurry, Yovo, hurry!" he pleaded.

Chapter Five

The old man was slight; it was easy for Kontu to push him along. But as they neared the waterfall, the rocks in the path were mossy and slimy and Kontu's own feet slid and faltered. More than once he and the priest both nearly crashed. Kontu prayed, but not aloud, for he knew no prayer that would make his arms stronger than they could be and his feet surer and his legs swifter. He simply prayed over and over, "Help us, help us, help us!"

The priest gasped and panted, Kontu was afraid he was killing him. He wished he knew which of the leaves the old man had taken from his pack and chewed earlier that day, the ones that had revived him. If he knew, he would take them from Yovo's bundle and they would both chew all of them, for never had he been any wearier or needed revival any worse. They had not eaten all day, and drunk only the drink Yovo had boiled for them in the chieftain's hut.

They were quite close to the falls now. The spray of water blowing over them made the rocks even slipperier, but it was cool and refreshing. The roar of the falls was worrisome to Kontu, for he couldn't hear any other thing, he could not know if the Primitives were close behind them. They must climb to the top before he let the old man rest. He whispered to him, words of encouragement that he was scarcely aware of speaking, "Just a little higher, Father Yovo. A step more and a step more."

He was himself half hypnotized by the sound of his own voice and went a step more and a step more on his weary legs, half carrying Yovo, not daring to look up and see how many more rocks and ledges loomed over them, and how far they would have to go. How they managed, he did not know but at last there was only one more ledge, higher than the priest's head, to scramble up and they would be at the top of the falls.

Kontu saw that he could climb it easily, there were broken places for his feet and tree roots for handholds, but he knew that he would have to push Yovo, and keep a firm grip on him, for the old man no longer had the strength to pull himself up such a wall. First, Kontu took the Sacred Pack from the priest's back and climbed up far enough to shove it well back from the edge. Then he jumped down and guided Yovo's hand to a root and his feet to the right places and prodded him along until at last the priest fell over onto the top of the rock ledge.

Kontu went weak with relief and stood balanced with his toes burrowed into cracks in the stone, clinging to the rock face, breathing hard, and trying to gather his strength again to haul himself up beside the old man. He had supposed that Yovo would lie still and wait for the boy to join him, take a moment to rest and breathe in the cool air. But the boy had forgotten that Yovo was a priest above everything else, and that his first thoughts were for the sacred objects in his bundle. When Kontu glanced up, the old man was already standing, the pack in his hands. Yovo tried to slip his arms into the straps, leaning backward, shaking with weariness, swaying back and forth.

He would fall! Yovo would fall, crashing down among the rocks below the waterfall. Kontu cried out and grabbed unthinkingly toward the old priest, almost losing his grip and falling himself.

The old man teetered at the edge and Kontu scrabbled at the rocks and went up more like a quick-climbing lizard than a boy. The blisters on his fingers were ripped open, his bare thighs and knees scraped and slashed by the rocks, yet he climbed frantically, unaware of anything but that tiny frail figure being pulled backward into the deep gorge by the Sacred Pack. He threw himself up over the sharp edge of the ledge and on his knees caught Yovo around the waist and they rolled together in the mud and loose rocks.

Yovo grunted and lay still, the pack slid from his arms and Kontu thought again that the old man was dying. But there was nothing he could do and he lay staring up into the deepening twilight sky and trying to silence his panting. No birds called here and the toad he had heard earlier had ceased to trill. There was only the sound of the falls in his ears and the furious thumping in his chest. But he must not forget the Primitives in spite of his weariness and his bruises and his aching lungs.

He crawled to the edge and peered into the dimness below. The little men were spewing from the woods, shapes in the dusk.

He and Yovo could not outrun them, he knew that now. Something would have to be done. And it was he, Kontu, who must do it. This morning he had taken part in a great magic and been vouchsafed a vision. Tonight, surely the spirits that had been with him then would be with him now and still the wildness of his heart and the tearing of his breath so that he could think of some way of escape. Yovo's magic had helped them escape the Primitives' camp, now Kontu's magic must save them.

There around him lay all the piled up dry trash brought along by high waters over the years, uprooted bushes and broken limbs and dried grasses and leaves. It was bunched along the rocky banks and caught against the rotting log at the head of the falls. Surely one skinny boy and one wizened old man could hide amongst that debris for a few hours and fool the Primitives? But where? His eyes darted frantically from one brush heap to another. Where?

And suddenly, in the fading rays of the sun, the whole ridgetop blazed in a soft reddish glow and it seemed to Kontu that he and the piles of trash around him were afire, were caught in a great burning sent by the powerful Fire Spirit to end their existence in white flakes of ash. A shout from below reminded him that he was seeking a hiding place and that he had better be quick about it.

Then he saw. He cried out, "Fire! Fire will save us! The girl said the Primitives feared Fire!" The spirits had not forsaken him but had sent him a message of deliverance. For Fire was the friend of all Adena people and would come to his aid. The idea gave him new hope and new courage and new strength.

He turned toward the priest and wrenched the Sacred Pack from him and began to loosen the top from the bowl of hot coals. The thought came to him as he worked that perhaps Fire might fail him now, as he had failed it earlier in the day when he let it fall to the hut's floor. Still, it was his only chance.

He would offer a prayer to Fire later, for time was precious. Snatching the cover from the bowl he blew on the coals and when they were red-hot lit a piece of dry moss. This he tossed into a branch covered with dead withered leaves. It blazed at once and with this torch he went from trash pile to trash pile, lighting each. Now taking a long forked stick he began to push and shove and roll the nearest burning logs and limbs and masses of grass toward the ridgetop path.

The brush burned and crackled and roared and great

flames leaped out at him as he prodded with his stick. Fire was the strongest thing; he had not really known before how strong. It scorched his torn hands and his arms, he could scarcely bear the heat against his cheeks and eyes. Still he worked on furiously.

And then he stopped and peered cautiously down the path. There they were—little dark scrambling wild things —swarming over the slippery rocks. Suddenly they seemed to become aware of Kontu and the red glow haloed around him. They stopped, unsure, waiting. In the half-light he could almost see the fearsome tattooed faces and angry eyes lit by the fire behind him.

With his forked stick he pushed pile after pile over the edge, heard the burning logs go thudding over the rocks, and then the terrified cries of the Primitives warriors. More and more burning trash he shoved down the path, till at last all he had accumulated here was gone. He wiped the sweat from his face and ran his bleeding hands over the parched skin of his arms. Then he once again looked over the edge and pride and exultation flooded through him at the sight. The Primitives were fleeing, all who had escaped the shower of sparks and flaming debris. A burning log had pinned one of the little dwarfs against a rock, and others beat at their blazing hair and knocked embers from their bodies as they ran. He watched till the last of them dodged through the flames into the dark pine woods.

He went back to the old man, still lying on the ground, and began to put the Fire Bowl back into its place on the priest's pack. "There was no time for prayers to Fire," he said. "It was wrong . . . but . . . I was frightened . . . they were almost to the top. . . ."

Yovo sat up but did not answer. Kontu tried to think of something else to say. He wished Yovo would make some comment about whether he was right or wrong.

The log caught at the edge of the waterfall was blazing

now, and the debris piled behind it was burning too. Those in the camp below needed to be reminded of the power of the Adena and of the Adena's constant friend, Fire. Kontu raked the trash into the stream and it turned to flame and went over the edge. With a long pole he tried to loosen the huge log balanced at the edge. He was shaking with weariness and his arms had little strength in them, but he kept prying and shoving till finally the dead tree moved and gave way.

Clinging to the rim of the cliff he looked down. The pool at the base of the ridge glowed and blazed in the dark, an awesome sight which must have filled the Primitives in the camp with great fear—Fire that fell from the sky and made the river burn—adding another curse to those horrors of illness and death they already endured. Perhaps now, Kontu thought, these people would leave and go to some other place and better luck would befall them. But he could not care. He could only rejoice that he had for the moment escaped them and saved Yovo and given the priest the chance to go on seeking the Eye and save the Adena. It was a great thing for a novice of the priesthood to achieve.

The daylight faded and still he and Yovo sat and rested. A little moon rose and the eerie bird that wept along the night streams and cried its name over and over came and crouched below them among the rocks, calling and calling. Kontu knew they must go on, but he could not summon the strength. He wished there was something for them to eat before they traveled on. But Gunt had all their food.

"Get up, Kontu," the priest spoke and his voice was stronger. "Hurry, hurry. We must find Gunt and Watota."

It was Yovo's scolding tone he used every morning to get Kontu out of bed and traveling. The boy rose slowly. There was a long way ahead of them. He thought of home and was sorry that he had set out on this journey. Here and now he should tell Yovo that he did not want to be a priest. It was much too difficult. He would ask Yovo to let him drop his ritual duties and go back to his town. No matter that since childhood his head had been molded and flattened by boards and cords into its priestly shape. No matter the number of prayers and rituals he had already learned.

But the old man walked off before he could speak. Kontu stood a moment and then hurried after him. They went along the path in the moonlight, the old man trembled and stumbled, but he did not ask to stop and rest and Kontu held him up as best he could. They paused once, crossing the flat top of the ridge, and then they were cautiously feeling their way down the other side toward the camp. Kontu peered ahead at each turn of the path. Surely soon there would be a campfire and the gleam would show among the trees and guide them to the place.

But there was no fire. Perhaps it had died while the warriors and their guards slept. Perhaps he and Yovo had passed the place. But no, faint light shone on the twisted pine to one side of the path. He had noticed it when they passed in the morning. He stopped and whispered to Yovo. "We are very close," he said. "And there is no fire."

"I know,'" Yovo answered. "It is queer. But we will go on."

They found the clearing and the camp with no trouble. The ashes of the fire were cold. There was no sign of Watota or Gunt or the Primitives; no packs, no weapons, nothing. The old man and the boy stood in the moonlit clearing and all around them were the sounds of little winds and the voices of crickets and the dark and nothing more.

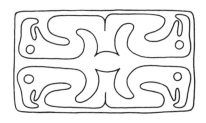

Chapter Six

"We must not stay here," whispered Yovo and Kontu agreed, while his eyes searched the thick shadows at the edge of the clearing. Whatever had happened to Gunt and Watota could easily happen to them. They would go on through the moonlit forest and sleep somewhere else.

They did not go far. Yovo could no longer walk. Near a stream they came upon great hemlocks whose branches swept the ground. Under one of them Kontu made a bed of moss and needles and the old man crept upon it and was asleep almost at once. Kontu lay awake listening to Yovo's breathing and the sounds of insects: *Ditty chiddle ditty chiddle*—over and over. As long as they went on calling he knew no enemy was approaching.

He was hugely tired and hungry; his torn and burned fingers stung and ached. He could not sleep, but he must, he knew. He must be rested for whatever tomorrow might bring. He said a prayer for safety over and over and drew himself deeper and deeper inside his own mind until suddenly he was asleep.

When he awoke it was long past first birdcall, even under the mourning shadow of the hemlock he knew that. The sun was high and the day sounds loud and busy all around. He sat up and looked for Yovo, but the old priest was not there. He scrambled up and out from under the tree. He would go to the river for his morning bath and prayers and start the day in proper fashion before he looked for the old man. Today, even though he had risen late he would do all things as they should be done, in order not to anger any of the spirits.

He made his way down the bank and saw Yovo walking along the other side of the little river, looking for something among the rocks and ferns. They did not speak, and Kontu waded out into the water and performed his morning ritual. When it was done and he stood naked and dripping, the priest crossed to him and held out some leaves.

"For your hands," Yovo said. He made a poultice of the crushed leaves and some mud and spread it over Kontu's burns. The boy sat, holding his hands stiffly out in front of him, while the priest washed the roots and sprouts he had gathered for their breakfast. He turned over rocks and caught two big crayfish and some snails. They would eat at least. Not well, perhaps, but Kontu was so hungry he could have eaten the very rocks on which he sat. Anyway, Adena were never squeamish about food. What the earth spirits supplied, they ate. It was awkward feeding himself with his mud-caked hands, but he managed and wished for more. Gunt's snakes seemed a feast, and a long time ago.

When they had eaten and Kontu had dressed, the old man picked up their packs and fastened his on his own shoulders and then helped Kontu settle his. They made their cautious way back to the camp. Once more they found no sign of the hunters or the Primitives. In the daylight the empty clearing was as forbidding as in the dark. It was strange. Yovo stood for a while quietly looking down at the ashes of the fire, and then he said, "Come. We must go on."

Kontu stared. Go on? The priest was addled. Yesterday's

horrors had driven him mad. Or the evil that had dwelt in that hut had entered into Yovo and twisted his heart. Go on, without the hunters and their axes and throwing sticks and spears? Go on without someone to bear the extra burdens of food or to prepare the skins and furs they would need when the cold weather came? Yovo was mad!

The priest glanced at his novitiate.

"I have prayed and I have fasted." He smiled a little grimly. "The answer revealed to me is plain. We have come this far and have been brought safely through a great danger. We must go on. If I should die along the way, then that will be a sign you must turn back. But while I breathe . . . live . . . we go on!"

Kontu bent his head. He had no choice. He had to go with the old man, if only to look after him. That the mission was a great and good one he already knew. In his heart he had known that it was a thing Yovo was willing to give his life for. In the end it might cost both their lives. But what were their lives compared to the good of all the Adena people? Two lives weighed against the well-being of so many. He should not have doubted.

He followed Yovo once more to the trail and they set out down the valley, winding back and forth across the rocky stream. Kontu walked on legs a little stiff and sore from the strain of pushing the logs and brush over the edge of the waterfall; he was still hungry, his hands were still painful. But he thought of the Eye, shut and withholding its power from his people; he thought of Fire and Snake and Eagle, who had somehow turned away from the Adena, and how he must not fail in the effort to bring them back. He thought of Yovo's courage and he prayed and walked and prayed and walked and tried not to feel.

Suddenly Yovo gave a cry and Kontu jumped and looked wildly around. The old priest bent down by the edge of the path and held up triumphantly a wad of strange leaves. "Here is what I have been searching for," he said. "These will do much more for your burns than the ones I found this morning."

They came soon to a trickle of water and Yovo washed the mud from Kontu's hands and bound the new wet leaves on them with strands of grass. Kontu thought that it was not so much the leaves that helped his hurts as the idea that the old man had been looking for this plant to ease the boy's pain, not just blindly following the trail, as Kontu had been doing.

At any rate he felt better at once, and they rested a few moments and discovered bushes covered with berries, sweet and juicy. Kontu did not pick them but held up the briery branches and bit the berries off in juicy mouthfuls. It was easier and quicker that way. It made Yovo laugh.

"You are half raccoon," he said. And Kontu's heart lightened further. Surely Yovo did not think too badly of him, in spite of the mistakes he made yesterday. Perhaps the old priest still had hopes for his pupil. Kontu longed for a word of praise for his actions in saving the two of them from the Primitives, but at least Yovo was not displeased with him.

When they began their journey once again, Kontu tried to keep his eyes open for any signs of danger and his ears listened for any tell-tale sounds. Without the hunters, who else would stay on the alert for danger? He did not believe the Primitives would follow or attempt revenge, but the mystery of the disappearance of Gunt and Watota and their guards gnawed away at his nerves and helped to keep him watchful.

For two days they walked and nothing happened and there was no sign of any other human. Kontu was hungry all the time and ate anything he could find, roots and berries, a fish caught in a puddle left by a drying stream, lichen and mushrooms, lizards and insects. He shared all these things with Yovo as a matter of course, but the old man did not seem to suffer as he did.

Perhaps a boy's stomach was bigger, Kontu thought, or perhaps the gravity of their errand took up so much of Yovo's thoughts he had no room for hunger. But whenever a deer leaped across the path, Kontu told himself that if he could have chased and killed it, he could have eaten the animal all by himself without troubling to skin or cook it.

Toward the end of the second day while they looked for a place to sleep, Kontu turned suddenly and looked down the path behind him. What had made him turn he did not know, some sound not quite heard, some feeling that his mind barely caught. A shadow slipped away in the undergrowth. Was that another deer? A wolf? A witch come to steal their breath away? Anything at all?

He said nothing to Yovo and he did not investigate. But on the next day's march he kept a grim watch and turned often to stare down the trail or deep into the forest on either side. At the top of rises he scanned every open space. At every bend in the route he stepped into the bushes and crept through the brush to peer back the way they had come. Yovo seemed indifferent to these precautions and walked steadily on.

They followed a narrow valley that seemed to concentrate the heat of the sun. The trees were sparse and the undergrowth scraggly. The stony path suddenly split ahead of them. One branch led straight on through the valley, the other climbed the low hill to the west. Kontu was glad when Yovo without hesitation took the route leading up the hill. He wanted to leave the suffocating little gulley behind. Besides from the ridge crest he could look back a great way and surely be able to spot in that thin woods anyone or anything that had been following.

The slope was gentle; they reached the top easily. Kontu turned. He searched the valley and saw nothing. Not a thing moved, nothing seemed out of place. And yet he was still uneasy. Somehow he felt that something watched him carefully, though he could not detect where the feeling was coming from or what kind of thing emitted it. It was simply a feeling. The way down the other side was steeper and the path even stonier and harder to travel. Kontu worried that Yovo would slip and kept close beside him.

They had almost reached the bottom when there was a noise behind them. A small round stone skipped and rattled and bounded down the path. Kontu clutched his knife and felt the stiff scabs crack along the joints of his fingers.

"Someone is following us," he whispered to Yovo. "I felt it yesterday and today, and now I know."

The old man shrugged. "Perhaps. It may have been an animal that loosened the rock. Or something we did ourselves when we passed that way. It may be that someone is following us. But can you think of any reason why they would? Perhaps they mean to do us harm, perhaps not. In either case there is not much we can do about it, is there?"

The priest turned his back on Kontu and stumbled down the last few steps of the descent. Kontu followed. It was not the Primitives, he was certain. By now he would have seen some sign of them, or they would have attacked. It was not an animal; it was a person or a witch-spirit who observed them from hiding. An animal, hidden and watchful, gave one a different sensation.

That night he put the Sacred Packs close between himself and Yovo, held his knife ready in his hand, and determined to stay awake and keep watch.

But it was useless. Even though he propped his back against a tree and tried flexing his burned palms so the pain would keep him awake, his eyes drooped and he slept.

He awoke very early, as a priest should, by first birdcall.

A bird was stirring over his head, and the morning light was making a gray fire in the eastern sky and Kontu yawned. They were safe; no one had killed them in the night. He turned his eyes in the twilight toward the Sacred Packs and then he screamed. Both packs were gone!

Chapter Seven

Yovo staggered to his feet. "What is it?" he asked shrilly. "What troubles you?"

Kontu could not bring himself to answer. The pipes, the skull bowl, the Sacred Fire—gone, gone! Here they were, an old man and a boy far from home, weaponless and helpless. Only the magic in the holy bundles had held danger at bay, had offered them protection. And now that too was gone.

"What is it?" Yovo asked again more calmly, seizing Kontu by the shoulders.

"The Sacred Packs!" quavered Kontu. "The packs are gone! Oh, Father Yovo, I tried to stay awake in the night to guard them. I knew someone followed us and was near, watching. But I fell asleep, and now all our magic is gone."

The old man stared at him. Kontu knew that it was worse for Yovo than for him. All Yovo's life was tied up in those skin parcels. Everything in them was worn from the touch of his hands, the countless times he had picked them up and laid them down, in love and honor. They were all his and yet they were not his; they belonged to the Adena people and had been given into his trust. If Yovo and Kontu should be able to make their way home without these things, the High Priest would certainly order Yovo's death for this negligence, and Kontu's also, since master and novitiate were as one.

Kontu watched the old man and saw in his eyes the struggle to stay tranquil and accept his fate whatever it might be.

The early light began to shine between the leaves of the trees. A robin called and another, farther away, answered. And then a human voice spoke, a voice Kontu knew. "The packs are here. They are safe."

It was the girl, the one who had translated for them in the hut of the leader of the Primitives. She squatted on the ground and the packs lay open before her, all the contents revealed.

At first Kontu could not believe his eyes, he simply stood and watched as she handled all the consecrated things. And then with a shout he started toward her, but Yovo put out a restraining hand. She settled everything into each pack and bound them up properly. The old priest and the young priest watched. The old man's hand on Kontu's shoulder trembled violently.

She picked up Yovo's pack and handed it to him. "Here, Grandfather," she said sneeringly. "I've done no harm."

Yovo took the bundle gently in his hands. "Daughter," he said sternly, "you have indeed done harm. These holy things are powerless without the guiding hand and knowledge of the priest. They could not harm you but you have harmed them. The spirits see this blasphemy you have committed. They will not take it lightly. They may very well wreak vengeance on us all because of you."

The girl shrugged. She went back and retrieved Kontu's bulky wallet and held it out to him. "Be careful," she taunted. "A witch-raven will jump out and take it away from you."

"Why did you do such a thing?" thundered Yovo. He

looked fierce and angry and made Kontu afraid. But the girl was not afraid.

"I wished to see," she answered evenly. "For a long time I have wanted to see the things that men call magic and that they use for healing and such things. And now I have." She smiled a little. "And now I have. Grandfather, I meant to be gone before you knew. I did not expect that one—" she nodded contemptuously at Kontu—"would wake so soon."

Kontu glared. He hated her.

Yovo still looked severe. "Did you not think the spirits would know, even if we did not?" he asked.

"Spirits?" the girl repeated. "What are spirits? Anyway, what have I to fear? All my life I have been a slave, beaten and hungry and made to work at the vilest tasks." She raised her arms and Kontu saw how they were scarred and bruised. She shrugged. "Do the spirits love me? Then let them hate me, and perhaps my life will be better."

Yovo and Kontu were silent, shocked. Finally Yovo turned to his follower and said, "We will not travel today. The cleansing ritual must be carried through, very very carefully. Perhaps twice, to make sure that all is done properly. This is a grave thing that has happened." He set out at once for the spring they had found the night before.

Kontu nodded and picked up his bundle. It was a grave thing. He moved off, heavy-hearted. Their misson was surely doomed, so many bad things had happened. And that girl! He could not understand her—to follow them out of curiosity to handle the sacred things when she could have traveled far from here by now, free as a breeze. He hoped that on the trail snakes would devour her or lightning strike her.

The ceremony went on and on through the morning and into the afternoon. Kontu put all thoughts of the girl firmly from his mind and followed all the prayers and songs carefully, not just saying the words over, as he often did, but thinking of them, concentrating on them, asking Eagle and Water and Fire to make all holy again.

When it was done, Yovo looked at him with an air of pleasure, as if he realized how much the boy had exerted himself.

It was late in the day when all was finished and the cleansed packs retied. There were still several hours of light remaining; however, Yovo thought they should not go on. The ceremonies were tiring and it was best to stay where they were and give the spirits time to calm themselves and receive the gifts of prayer and tobacco and penitence. And there was food to find for they had not eaten since the night before.

They walked back to their campsite—and the dreadful girl was still there. She seemed perfectly well, no snakes had bitten her or plague fallen on her. She was a horrible sight, true enough—dirty and scarred, her hair matted and full of burrs, her leather apron grimy and greasy.

Yovo glowered at her. "Why are you here?" he asked coldly. "You should have left this place. You are a danger to us."

"I am a help to you, Grandfather," answered the girl. She gestured toward the woods' edge where a young deer hung from a limb, gutted and skinned and beheaded. A little fire blazed nearby and on the ground were a spear and some knives. "You need me. I can hunt as well as any man. I can make a knife or spear and use it better than this boy."

Yovo hesitated. For the first time Kontu looked a little more kindly on the girl. The red juicy carcass hung shiny and inviting. It was a worthy gift for all the trouble she had caused. He hated to think that she could hunt better than he could, but the thought of eating deer meat for supper made him almost faint. Even Yovo by this time must need more than berries and snails.

The old priest looked sharply at the girl. "Then why do you need us?" he asked at length. "You can take care of yourself, you can travel safely alone. Why would you want to help us?"

She looked away then and Kontu saw sadness in the line of her cheek and chin. "Years ago, I lived in a village south and west of here," she said, squatting on her heels. "My mother and I were captured when I was only a baby. When I was three years old, she died, for our captors did not treat us well and she gave most of her food to me, I think. I was traded to another town, and I was not even then a good slave or afraid, and I was beaten and spat upon. Four times I was traded, and three times I escaped and was brought back, but I was alone in the forest long enough to know how to get along. I watched all the time when warriors flaked stone for spears and knives, and when I could I practiced and learned how. I can do almost anything." Her voice was boastful and Kontu grimaced, hating her and her cleverness.

"Now I have got away from that terrible village and the quarrelsome little people who lived there," she said and stood before Yovo. "I would like to go home now, to try to find the place where I came from. When I saw you, Grandfather, I knew you were kind. The Adena are good people. I thought I might help you and I thought I would like for a while to be with people who would not burn me with coals or cut me with knives, just because I was proud and would not in my mind be a slave, however much my body might be."

Yovo gazed at her thoughtfully. At last he sat down by the fire and lit his tubular pipe with the duck-bill lips. It was the second best pipe to offer tobacco and smoke to the spirits and Yovo smoked it whenever sacrifice and prayers were needed, but it was not a pipe for use inside Adena temples. He puffed in silence for a few moments, then he said slowly, "If while I sit here three doves fly overhead, it will be a sign and you may travel with us."

They sat quietly. The girl looked passive and dull-eyed. Kontu could not look away from the deer and could not think of anything else but the meal he might—or might not—get. But he heard right away the sweet whistle of wings when it sounded, and he glanced up to see them go over, one, two, three, and then no more.

He was astounded. The spirits sometimes acted in strange ways. So quick and easy an answer.

Yovo stood up and smiled. "Very well, Daughter," he said. "You will go with us. What is your name?"

"Neeka," she answered.

"Neeka, will you come to the river and wash all your yesterdays away, so that you may travel with us newborn, as Kontu and I are newborn from the waters?"

For a moment she looked puzzled and then she looked hesitant. But suddenly she shrugged and said, "Yes, Grandfather."

And they went. Kontu stayed by the fire and soon had slices of deer roasting on stones and cane spits. He could not wait but ate bits of the meat raw. His head was full of strange thoughts. He did not like this girl, who could kill a deer and do any other thing she liked. But he too saw that she would be a help to them. Or perhaps she would not. Perhaps she was indeed a witch come to them in human form. Or was playing some trick on them. Or would injure them in some way, stealing the packs and going off with them for good.

Perhaps Father Yovo should have asked for another sign. This time of year the woods were full of doves, as he and the priest both well knew. And yet, he pondered, those three doves had come, before the pipe of tobacco was half gone. It must be a sign.

When Yovo and the girl returned, Neeka looked more respectable. Her hair dripped with water and the burrs and tangles were mostly gone. She was clean, and her apron had lost some of its filth. She was clean, but she was not newborn. In her eyes there was still the gleam of haughtiness and bitterness and hatred. Kontu could see it, if Yovo could not.

Still she had killed the deer and they were eating well and there would be food for a day or so to come. That night Kontu slept soundly and next morning awoke early and was glad to see that all was well and the sun shone upon them as they set out upon the path, he and Yovo with their packs and the girl with her weapons and with chunks of meat bundled in the deerskin. But whether he walked before the girl or behind her, he was conscious of her presence all the time. And he wondered what having her with them would do to their mission.

Chapter Eight

"We must go carefully," Yovo cautioned. "There are people about."

It was hardly startling news to Kontu. He had seen signs already that they were approaching some kind of habitation, and so had Neeka. She had not hunted yesterday or this morning, though the supply of meat was getting low. Instead she had stayed close to them, saying very little, not even looking at the other two. Kontu thought she seemed not so ill-tempered and unpleasant as when she had first joined them. Maybe it was because she had nothing to say.

Still she hardly seemed aware that Kontu was there, though up till now she had often spoken with Yovo about plants and their uses, about the kind of land that lay ahead of them, about the villages of the Adena beyond the Crystal River.

Kontu hated her. He could not help it. That she was able to take her spear and go out into the woods and come back with a deer or opossum for their supper, filled him with disgust for himself and hatred for her. When he ate the good roasted deermeat, he rejoiced that it was there, but the taste was not as sweet as it should be. If he had killed it himself. . . .

"Father Yovo," he said once, "a woman should not hunt

and bring meat to our cooking fires. Maybe we are wrong to let her travel with us. It may be that by accepting her help in our quest we are angering the gods and our mission will fail."

Yovo frowned. "The spirits gave a sign," he answered, a little fretfully.

A sign! Those three doves! In late summer woods doves flew about constantly. Sometimes Kontu thought Yovo had asked for such a sign because he was sure it would be given. He was ashamed of such a thought, but it crept into his mind nevertheless. But then the spirits must have meant for this to come about, that the two men should be dependent on a sour-faced girl. After all, priests were not meant to be hunters.

The next morning they did not follow the trail but went quietly through the woods, hoping to avoid the strangers whose home this was. A high cliff barred the way however and Yovo was not sure what to do.

"Go back to the path," Neeka said simply. "If we meet someone, we meet them, that is all."

"They will make you a slave again," sneered Kontu.

"And you also," she responded quickly.

Yovo felt that the strangers might be avoided by climbing up and over the rock bluff. So they followed along the foot of the cliff, looking for a way up, and came suddenly on the home of the strangers, an opening stretching back under the overhanging stones. Skins were piled against the back walls as beds. To one side a fire burned, the roof above it black with greasy soot. Three women moved about this rock shelter doing various tasks, and some children played along the edge of a creek that ran in front of the place.

The children spied the travelers first and cried out, pointing. The women stopped what they were doing and turned to look. One of them had been pounding something in a small hollow in a boulder, and the other two were heating stones in the fire. These were people as poor and ignorant as the Primitives, Kontu saw, but they did not seem angry or fearful, simply curious.

As the travelers walked closer, one of the women spoke to them. The words were mysterious to Yovo and Kontu, and even Neeka did not understand.

Yovo gave a sign that meant, Let us walk the same white path. The women fell silent and the children ran toward the back of the rock shelter and gazed out of the shadows at them. The three intruders stood staring back. By and by a man approached through the trees toward the homesite. He carried a short spear. It was not a throwing weapon, but one used to jab and kill at close quarters. The rabbit that dangled from his hand must have been caught in a snare, Kontu thought.

The priest greeted the man with the sign of peace and the man repeated the sign and muttered more of their mysterious words. All of them stood looking at one another. Kontu could smell the stew cooking in a large hole in the boulder where the woman pounded—evidently, like the Primitives, these people made no vessels and they warmed their stew by dropping the rocks now heating in the fire into the hole filled with meat and water. He felt sorry for these people and their backward ways.

At last Yovo turned to Kontu and Neeka. "We will go," he said. "But slowly."

So they left, walking slowly back the way they had come, not turning to look at the cave dwellers behind them. They made their way through the forest until they found the path again and took up their journey south.

"If the man had tried to kill us, would you have fought him with your spear, oh mighty hunter?" asked Kontu softly.

Neeka shrugged. "No, but if I had been able to run away

and leave you to his cruelties, I would have," she answered shortly. And she would have, Kontu knew. He wondered if she had been frightened. She had not shown it. He had been frightened, a little, but he did not think he had shown it.

They walked on, keeping to the trail. They met no one else, but for two days Neeka did not hunt. She stayed with them and they ate the last of the deermeat they carried, and roots and grass seeds. So she had been frightened after all, and did not want to meet any of those cave dwellers with their short wicked spears alone in the woods. Only near the end of the second day she left them for a while and came back without anything to show for her hunt.

"So," said Kontu impulsively, "you can do anything a hunter can do . . . even come back empty-handed."

"You will go to sleep no hungrier than I," she retorted, and Yovo said, "Let us have peace."

They walked on through the little ridges the next day and Neeka killed a turkey. And then in a few more days' travel they were in a different country, rolling open land dotted with little wooded knobs. They had left the steep ridges and rocky creeks behind.

They passed a herd of elk and Kontu invited Neeka to kill one for their supper. Yovo said crossly, "No, they are too big. We could not carry so much meat, but would have to leave it for the vultures. Try not to be stupid, Kontu."

Neeka said, "I would not trouble to kill one. Look there."

She pointed and Kontu saw the gray shadows of a pack of wolves slipping through the tall grasses. The wolves intended the humans no harm, but he would not wish to quarrel with them over an elk's carcass. By and by they came on the skeleton of a young elk, its bones scattered and marked by the wolves' teeth.

There were deer, too, and turkeys and other game, and

they ate well as they crossed the open land of tall sedge and blue and yellow flowers. One morning the sky was dark with wave after wave of passenger pigeons flying over with a roar of wings.

The ground was slippery and noisome with their droppings, and the three travelers could find no shelter from the foul rain but had to wait till the flock was gone and then find a stream to wash themselves and their belongings.

The next day the sky was dark again, with clouds this time, strange yellowish clouds and a high keening wind overhead and curious flat, breathless stillness near the ground. They looked for shelter; the storm would be terrible when it came, they knew. On the side of one of the little domed hills they crouched among the bushes and waited. The sky grew darker and the wind shrieked. Drops of water fell fitfully and then the black swirling funnel appeared, far off, veering back and forth across the flat land. Birds swept through the sky, and leaves and branches; a rabbit were tossed into the air like a piece of bark. The elk and deer scattered in dismay, running wildly in panic.

The terrible spiral came roaring toward them and Kontu was scared to look, pressing his face into the hillside. He had heard of such storms, had even seen the damage they had done, but he had not known it would be so fearsome and monstrous, not like a natural thing at all, like a horrible witch-demon. The ground trembled with its noise, the trees above them splintered, and the tall meadow grass lay flat in the wind.

And then as it was almost on them it suddenly vanished, whirled up into the sky and broke into pieces and was gone.

The rain fell in torrents now and the wind blew savagely, but the danger was over. Kontu sat up and put his head on his knees, while the rain pelted down, and he thought hard. Yovo took their deliverance from danger always to be a sign that the spirits approved of what they were doing. But all these dangers, all these encounters with trouble, however often escaped from, were they not warnings from the spirits?

Were not the spirit-beings saying, "Turn back, turn back! Next time we will not be so kind."

And bowed there Kontu suddenly felt himself picked up and taken far away, from the rain and the meadow and the company of the others. For a moment he found himself once again staring down into the Eye in the Forest, once again saw it dim and go out, once again saw the horrible hard excrescences along the hillside.

It was so vivid and so real that he sprang up with a yell. In the rain Yovo and Neeka looked at him in alarm. The rain poured down and he seated himself without saying anything. He would tell Yovo later what had happened. But Neeka was not to know. Not for anything would he tell her about the Eye or the things he knew about it. Yovo had told her only that they searched for a sacred place, long lost to the Adena. Kontu was glad she did not know.

The rain poured down and poured down and poured down. Trees and bushes offered no shelter from the torrent. The three of them huddled together, protecting the sacred bundles as best they could, on and on through the day. Kontu felt they were like wasps fallen into a pool and struggling to keep from drowning.

But at long last the rain slackened and finally was over; only a thin mist lay across the fields of beaten grass. The sun shone down through the haze occasionally, making small rainbows. The whole earth lay still and exhausted after the storm, and when Kontu glanced around at Yovo and Neeka, he saw that they were both fast asleep; they too were worn out by the storm.

He was glad to be the only one who was awake. He was glad to be the strong one, the one the rain and wind had not wearied beyond hope. Silently he stood up and walked away.

But then he crept back and took Neeka's spear from the ground where it lay beside her. He would hunt for their supper. True, there were dead birds to be had for the gathering here; likely the tornado had killed other animals they could eat. Nevertheless he would hunt. If he killed something, well and good, and if he did not that would be all right too. He could say he had taken the spear for protection against wolves or maddened elk.

He walked through the light fog, watching the sun break through more and more often and sparkle in the air. The muddy ground and wet grasses made walking difficult. He went slowly and enjoyed the moist air slowly brightening around him and the calls of birds, growing stronger and more frequent as they too recovered from the storm.

There was another sound off to his right. Not a bird sound. He went in that direction, listening hard.

The sound came again, louder, strange, hollow, not like any sound he had ever heard. His heart beat faster and his hand tightened on the spear. Should he go on? Should he turn back and not discover what it was? It might be a witch hiding under the flattened grass and piles of debris. Perhaps Yovo should deal with it.

But he did not turn back. He moved cautiously on and the noise came again, a wailing echoing sobbing call, bewildering and awful. It came from the ground, from almost beneath his feet. From a gaping hole in the earth right in front of him. Softly, clutching his weapon hard, Kontu crept forward to look in.

Chapter Nine

Kontu almost turned and ran. What kind of horrible creature howled and stumbled around at the bottom of the sinkhole?

The sun came out fiercely and in its brightness he saw that the thing had the legs and arms of a man, covered with mud and grass and debris, but arms and legs nevertheless. Only its head was strange, shapeless and awful, and out of it came those eerie noises.

And then suddenly Kontu burst out laughing. He laughed so hard he almost fell into the hole himself. He crouched in the mud at the edge of the sink and gasped with laughter. At the bottom of the pit the creature looked up and scowled.

"Kontu!" it cried. "Kontu, thanks be to Snake you are here! Get me out! Get me out!" Kontu rolled about in the grasses, roaring with laughter.

"Kontu!" the voice from the sinkhole cried sadly. "Do not leave. Get me out."

At last Kontu leaned over the edge again and extended a hand. Gunt seized it and climbed the wall of the pit and stood beside the boy on firm ground. He was coated with slimy mud and on his head for protection against the storm he wore the leather pack in which he had carried his possessions.

No sooner had he stood up than he turned around and leaped back into the hole. Once again, Kontu was afraid. This was perhaps not Gunt at all but some kind of witch-demon, popping in and out of the earth this way. But then he saw that Gunt was busily picking up his belongings, the scattered knives and spear points and dried meat, and was packing them once more into his leather bundle. At last he handed it to Kontu and once more was hauled up to the surface.

"Kontu," he panted. "We thought you must be dead. And Yovo? Is he well? Where is he?"

"He is well," said Kontu. "Come along. You will see."

He did not ask any questions. It was Yovo's place to hear Gunt's story and find out what had happened.

Yovo and Neeka were awake, the old man was looking around uneasily, worried about Kontu going off by himself. Neeka stared at her spear, swinging from Kontu's hand, but she said nothing. When Yovo spied the two of them, he cried out joyfully. "Gunt! Gunt! You are alive! The Sacred Father Eagle has spared you! Where is Watota? Is he coming? How did you get here? Are you well? What happened?"

Gunt looked bewildered and Yovo took him by the hand and led him to a grassy spot and made him sit down.

"Now tell us what happened and how you came here," he said gently. Yovo was wise. Questions always befuddled Gunt, he had to tell things slowly and in his own way. Kontu laid the spear on the ground, and Neeka snatched it up and put it with her knives.

Gunt stared at Neeka but he did not ask about her. Instead, he turned to Yovo and said, "We waited for you, there with the little men. We waited and waited until it was almost dark. And then an owl came and spoke to us out of the dim forest. We were afraid, but we did not move. And then another came and it too spoke. It called a name, over and over. And then more came and more, and they were all around. Some were not owls; they were spirits, and they talked and said words in a strange language. The little men were frightened and then we heard a noise like shouts in the distance and the guards ran, ran fast into the trees and disappeared."

He looked at Yovo in his simple way, waiting for the priest to doubt his story. But Yovo nodded and Gunt went on. "They had tied us again as soon as you left, but not very well, and we untied the ropes quickly and found our packs and weapons and ran too. We did not know where we were going, only we went a different way from the Primitives. And in the morning we located a path going in the right direction and we followed it."

Yovo looked pleased. Watota and Gunt had not turned back home, they had trusted him to keep on with his mission and to find them wherever they were. A priest's followers should always have such trust in him.

"We came to this place," Gunt continued, "where there were many springs of strange tasting water. Some of it boiled up black in color and some of it was red. We did not like it. There were many paths around these springs and we did not know which one to take. So we stayed here, for we decided that sooner or later you must come here; all trails seem to lead here, and it is easy to spy men coming and going. We have seen them ourselves, two hunting parties and a trader. There is game in plenty and we had a rest and ate well and waited. Then today was an evil day and the storm came."

He stopped, as if that was all he had to say and everything they might want to know. Yovo waited but at length he said, "Watota. What about Watota?"

Gunt shrugged.

"We hid from the storm," he said. "Among some trees along a creek. But the black sky demon came down and headed straight for us, rushed at us to tear us into bits and devour us. I ran. Watota could not keep up. I ran as fast as I could, and then all at once there was no ground under me and I was in a hole. The wind demon passed over and I was not harmed. But I thought I would drown. I thought the water would fill that place and drown me, in such a rain. I put my pack on my head and waited. But I was not drowned. I was saved."

He looked proud of himself, as though he had done something unusually clever. Perhaps it was not clever, Kontu thought, but no doubt running and falling into the pit had saved Gunt's life. He wondered if something equally fortunate had happened to Watota or whether the young hunter lay dead among the drowned grasses and scattered tree branches.

Gunt glanced now at Neeka for a second time. "You were saved too," he said at last, "the two of you. I thought you would die without someone to hunt for you. I hoped you would find a way here, but I was not certain. And now there are three of you."

Yovo gestured at Neeka. "A young woman who joined us," he explained. "She . . . she hunted for us."

For the first time he seemed a little reluctant to say it, Kontu noticed. But Gunt was not taken aback. Gunt, it occurred to Kontu, would always be one who was willing to let others be, let them hunt who liked to hunt, let those who simply liked to sit in the grass and enjoy the songs of grasshoppers do that.

It is because he is nothing, thought Kontu. He does not care what anyone is because he is nothing.

Yovo told of their escape from the Primitives. "It was Kontu who saved us," he ended up. "It was he who set the wood afire and pushed it over the waterfall and scattered the Primitives."

Kontu felt the girl's scornful look. He had been so pleased at the priest's words of praise. He had waited for them a long time. All these days he had waited for some word, to show that in spite of all his lacks and errors, Yovo was not disappointed and disapproving of him. And now it had come. Yovo thought him worthy.

And yet—and yet— At last he spoke. "It was Neeka who told us they so feared fire," he said in a low voice. And she is the one who has fed us, on the trail."

No one answered. Only Yovo stood up and fussily arranged his shirt and medicine bag and said, "Now we must eat and sleep, quickly. For we must be up early in the morning, and traveling fast."

The sky was filled with a harsh gold light even after sunset and Kontu could not sleep. He wondered about Watota. Would Yovo make no effort to find the young warrior? Was the old man in such a hurry because he believed he was going to die? Hurry, hurry. Yovo said it all the time. Winter is coming. Did he believe it was the long winter sleep of his own life ahead of him before they found the Eye?

A bat fluttered out and up into the darkening air, and Kontu slept.

They were up early, all of them, and soon on the southward path. Kontu had thought Yovo would at least go to the stream where Gunt and Watota had hidden since their arrival and look for the young Adena, call out his name, leave some sign for him. But no. They followed the winding path without a moment wasted. Still, Yovo behaved oddly. He searched for landmarks, as if he had been here before and knew where to go.

Gunt found a bear cub killed by a falling tree, and Yovo would scarcely wait long enough for him to gut it and skin it for their meal that night. Gunt had to leave the feet, of which he was especially fond when they had been roasted in hot ashes. Yovo pulled him away from the carcass to hurry onward.

They walked for two days and then dropped from the prairie land into a deep-forested river bottom, green and silent. They did not rush here, though the path was easy to follow, but paused often. Yovo seemed to be waiting for something to tell him where to go. He was like a fox who smelled something on the wind. And at last he led them beside a river pool, greeny-black and still as death; on its edge was a hollow sycamore tree, huge, gleaming silver and tan through the gloom of the leafy afternoon.

"Wait here," he said, when they got within a certain distance of the great tree. "Do not speak."

Kontu was puzzled and afraid, the others were indifferent. Whatever Yovo was up to did not matter to them. The girl sat down, and Gunt merely stood and stared.

Yovo walked up to the dark split in the sycamore tree.

"Are you there?" he called. "Come out at once!"

Kontu thought he must have taken leave of his senses, and then he heard something stir in the hollow bole of the tree.

"Come out!" commanded Yovo once more. After a while a face appeared at the opening. Watota! His eyes were wide with fear and madness, his mouth hung slack.

"Shape-changers!" he screamed. "Witches! Go away!" Go away!" He vanished again, crying out, "Witches!" and Yovo turned to the others.

"Yes, go away. Find a camping place and make ready something to eat. I will be with you when I have calmed him. Do not be alarmed. I have treated this illness before. It happens to a man too long alone in a strange place."

Kontu went with the others, though as the priest's assistant he had hoped to see what Yovo would do to restore Watota. It did happen to those who got lost, he knew, so that after a while they could not distinguish their friends from puffs of air, would not answer those who called to them, and hid at the approach of searchers.

Among the Adena there was a saying, A man is not alone in this world unless the priest withdraws his shield. He had heard often of men in a strange place and how something followed them, something watched them, wherever they went, so that they could never be free of fear and could not tell their friends from demons and died of fear and thirst and hunger within a hand's reach of rescue. It did not happen often, but then Adena warriors did not often go so far from home, so far into strange lands.

The storm must have frightened Gunt and Watota far worse than it had Yovo and Kontu, who had magic always with them and a straight pathway to the home of the spirits.

Kontu went with Neeka and Gunt and it occurred to him suddenly that Yovo had known Watota was ahead of them, driven by the fury of his lostness. The old man might have known even that Watota was hiding in a sycamore tree. From within himself the priest had seen out beyond them and found Watota. He, Kontu, would some-day be able to do such a thing.

Someday perhaps he would be able to have such priestly powers and use them to help his people. Let Neeka throw her spear and kill turkeys, like a man. Let her tongue whip across his pride and make him feel small. This she would never do. Magic would never be hers as it might some time be his.

They went downstream and built a fire and ate the bear cub meat and the rest of the sunflower tubers Neeka had found and baked yesterday. Kontu had never tasted a root so sweet and good. Why did she always seem to find the best things to eat and the best places to stay—she had no magic; she did not even believe in magic. Why should the gods favor her? he asked himself worriedly.

At last Yovo appeared, leading Watota and they came and sat by the fire. At first Watota seemed jumpy and uneasy, but when he had eaten and listened to the others talk and felt the heat of the fire, he grew much calmer. He even spoke a little, describing how he had killed a deer with one antler and had been chased from his prey by wolves.

"We will hear that tale more than once," Kontu muttered. "And others too."

Watota asked no questions, glancing at the girl but appearing scarcely to see her. Yovo must have given him some drug for he soon fell asleep, as did the old man. The other three sat talking among themselves around the fire.

They talked about the sunflower tubers and how the girl had come to know about them, to recognize them, and to learn how to cook them. "It was when I was very young and a long way from here," she explained. "It was lucky for me. I ran away and was in the woods a long time and these were what I had to eat for many days."

She nodded scornfully at the sleeping Watota. "I was not afraid like that one," she said. "I was only afraid of being caught again. And I was," she added gloomily.

"Then it was different for you," said Gunt. "It was different."

He went off under a tree and lay down. Neeka moved away too.

But Kontu sat on for a long time, gazing into the fire and thinking about how strange the world was, full of things of which only the spirits knew the cause. And only the priests surely might hold the strangeness at bay and shield the others from it.

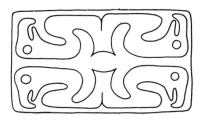

Chapter Ten

"It is wrong," said Watota solemnly. "A woman hunting is wrong. The spirit of deer and the spirit of grouse and the spirit of rabbit, they will have their revenge on us for letting her use a spear."

Yovo looked uneasy, as he often did when the subject was brought up—and Watota brought it up often. But the priest said nothing.

Kontu said nothing, staring back into the cave where the rock walls and ceiling and the dusty floor funneled into a small, round, black mystery. There were bear tracks in the dust. But the hole was much too small for a bear to enter. It must have come into the cave looking for mice or grubs, and gone out again.

Gunt said nothing. So Watota went on, speaking gravely and angrily. "We will not accomplish our mission. Evil will befall us. Why, she says no prayer to the hunting spirits before killing nor a prayer of thanks to the deer when it falls to her spear."

Yovo grimaced. But Gunt spoke up suddenly. "Yet the deer do fall to her spear. She has killed two, and you only one." Gunt had killed nothing himself, he had not even gone hunting more than once or twice since he returned to the party. He searched for fruits and nuts and gathered seeds, but he did not take a throwing stick and spear and go looking for game.

"Besides," he went on, "we did not have the greatest luck before she came among us, did we? And we followed the hunting rituals too. Things have gone badly from the first, girl or no girl." He paused. "It would not be the first time men have failed to please the gods, no matter how hard they tried."

Yovo glared at Gunt. Kontu thought perhaps the old man felt that saying such a thing was bad, and was a challenge to the gods to wreak havoc on them. But more than that it was not for Gunt, a warrior, to interpret what the spirit world ordained. That was best left to priests.

Kontu turned the matter over in his mind. The presence of the girl worried him too, in many ways. Yet Yovo had asked for and been given a sign. The gods looked with favor on the priest. They had given him the means of saving the Adena from the Primitives and had bestowed on him the power to find Watota, who might otherwise have died, mad and alone.

Kontu took off his deerskin shoe and inspected the thin place in the sole. In another day's walking it would wear through. He must think about making new ones. "I must have a new shoe," he said to no one in particular, holding up the mocassin.

Neeka wandered into the cave. She had been to a nearby stream to bathe and drops of water stood all over her bare body.

"There!" Watota growled. "There is a task for her. A woman's task, making shoes."

She whirled on him so that the water from her hair flew in a circle about her and hissed softly into the little fire on the dirt floor. "If I make shoes for you, I will make them out of your own hide," she cried. Her eyes burned with anger. "I choose my tasks. If any of you think that is bad, say so, and I will travel alone. I kill my own meat and make my own shoes and I stay here only as long as I am welcome."

Watota started up, angry too. He looked as though he might strike her. Gunt stood quickly.

"I will make the shoes," Gunt put in. "I have a skin already softened and I will make the shoes. I will get other skins ready too, in case we should need them."

Yovo said, "Let us have peace among ourselves. Come, Kontu, we will have prayers."

Kontu was sorry to go in one way; he enjoyed somehow seeing Watota be Neeka's victim, rather than himself. But in a way, he hated it when any of them quarreled. It was wrong and it bothered him. Of them all, he thought suddenly, it was Gunt who never got angry or seemed distressed by any of it, who always smoothed things over.

It is because he is nothing, Kontu told himself.

He followed Yovo from the cave. They walked in a mysterious country full of caves and sinkholes. Streams of water disappeared, suddenly and entirely, into the ground. Sometimes Kontu leaned over one of the sinkholes and heard the sounds of water running. Under their feet, under the solid earth and the grasses and ferns, the ground was full of holes and rivers and tunnels and rooms. It made him shiver. Perhaps it was like that everywhere and only showed itself here. Perhaps every time a man put his foot upon the path he was walking not on solid earth but on a thin cover over empty air and darkness.

He knew this was not so. He had often seen slaves digging pits into the ground for certain kinds of stones, and he had seen how solid and how deep the earth was. But all these caves, blowing their cool breath out into the summer air, gave him odd ideas.

The next morning on the trail, Watota, who was leading the way, stopped suddenly. "See," he called out. "See the tree there with the lightning scar? The big white spot on the trunk? I can hit it with my spear."

He took his throwing stick with its upright notch at the end and placed the butt of his spear shaft against the notch. Gripping the handle of the throwing stick, he balanced the spear above it with his thumb and first finger. The spear was firmly seated against the notch. He drew back his arm and threw, the throwing stick sent the spear forward and straight toward the scarred tree. It whistled through the air in a long beautiful arc and struck the tree trunk just at the lower edge of the white mark.

Watota laughed aloud. "Let us see you match that," he taunted Neeka. "Let us see you hit the mark, oh, she who hunts!"

For a moment Neeka said nothing. She walked on, gripping her spear. And then she said dryly, "I use my spear for hunting, not for playing games."

Yovo said a little impatiently, "She could not match you, Watota. She does not have your strength, she has no throwing stick."

Gunt said, "She can kill a deer."

Watota stared furiously at all of them. He had to fetch his spear from the tree. When he came back to the trail, he was far behind them and made no effort to catch up.

The day went by, hot and dry. Since the storm no rain had fallen and the paths grew dusty. Sometimes in the afternoons clouds, black and heavy, appeared along the edge of the sky, thunder rumbled far off. The travelers were often thirsty, for streams were few and many of them had dried to a muddy trickle. The meadows stretched around them, covered with waist-high bronze grasses, and trees were scattered. Their passing sent grasshoppers whirring up, but only Gunt was interested; he caught and munched them as he moved along.

Once they came on a grisly sight. A high scaffolding supported a platform and on the platform lay the dead bodies of men and women, naked and putrefying. Kontu was frightened, for there was an unnatural stillness here he did not like. But Yovo nodded his head.

"We will go by quietly," he ordered. "This is a sacred place. Some people do this thing, expose the bodies of their dead high in the air, so that birds and winds and sun and rain can remove all the flesh from the bones. Then they gather the bones and bundle them together with thongs and bury them."

"Why do they do a thing such as that?" asked Watota. He was shocked. Kontu was shocked too. The Adena people laid their dead decently in the earth, along with their possessions, covered them carefully, so that all might quickly leave this world and go to the next.

"They are ignorant," said Yovo. "It is the way of an ignorant people." They walked by with averted heads, only Neeka turned to look at the platform black against the sky.

The weather grew hotter and drier and even the nights were hot and roared with the noise of insects. The party followed the path wearily. It seemed to Kontu that the landscape was always the same, as if they moved their legs up and down and never got anywhere, only somehow stood in the same place. The sun burned down, at noon they found what shade they could and often rested for a while. Yovo made a bonnet of leaves and wore it on his head. Insects swarmed around their faces and flew into their eyes. Though they had no trouble finding food, cooking and eating seemed almost more bother than it was worth, and Yovo grew thin and gaunt.

Kontu worried. Were they in a land where the new spirits were more powerful than those of the Adena? Would Yovo's magic work here to save them from whatever evil might befall them?

He lay awake during the nights, listening to the sounds of wind and birds and the steps of a deer running not far off. Stars fell in a shower through the sky, like sparks flying up when a new log was thrown on the fire. It was the time of year for shooting stars, he knew that. It would have been more strange if it had not happened. Yet it made him uneasy. Suppose in this land the stars fell all the way to earth and one of those burning things should slide straight down on top of them. He wished they could sleep in rock shelters or caves.

They went on. Day after burning day went by and then there were more trees around them and in their shade the undergrowth was not so brown and brittle, the dust not so choking and thirst-making, but the gnats and flies were worse. The trail led them among more and bigger trees, into a real woodland, dim and green. Kontu felt better among the big trunks and the swooping grapevines. Some of the grapes were ripe and he ate them eagerly, as did the others.

Neeka ate more than any of them, running ahead to look for them on the ground. "When I was a slave, I was not allowed to eat grapes," she told Kontu.

He had forgotten that Neeka had ever been a slave. It was strange to think of so fierce a spirit being bound. No wonder she had been so resentful of Watota's orders to make shoes, after so many years of being compelled into obedience. For the first time, he wondered what it must be like never to be free but always doing as one was told to do. He always did Yovo's bidding, it was true, but because he wanted to, not because he was forced to.

Then quite suddenly the path ended. It was there ahead of them and then it was not. It disappeared into the ground like one of those streams they had passed in the cave country. They scouted through the undergrowth looking for it, but found no trace.

"We will go back," said Yovo. "There was a fork we missed perhaps."

They walked all the way to the edge of the woods but found no division in the trail. Yovo stood thinking. He walked away from the others through the meadow grasses, looking here and there. Suddenly he called out and beckoned sharply to the others, and they came running.

The priest had found a rattlesnake, a small one, fat and lazy. A rattlesnake, the father of all snakes and possessing great power in this world and the world of the spirits. When they came close, the snake coiled. Its tail tipped with small rattles whirred like the wings of a fly trapped in a spiderweb.

"A stick, a stick," cried Yovo. "I need a stick."

But there were no sticks, not here in the grasses. Kontu was preparing to run back to the woods when Neeka handed the old man her spear. He grasped it wrong way around, just below the stone point. He went toward the snake speaking soft words to it.

"Friend and helper, mighty spirit, show us the way," he breathed. "Do not harm us, help us, for we are brothers."

Suddenly he shoved the handle of the spear under the coils and tossed the snake into the air. It landed wriggling in the grass. "After it, after it!" Yovo cried and they ran following the snake. And by and by they came to a new trail, skirting the woods altogether.

"Snake is never lost," explained Yovo. "He will always show you the way if you do not harm him. But if you ask him the direction in that manner, you must be very careful.

Never get too close. Snake is not trustful and does not always know friend from foe."

By afternoon they had reached the banks of a large green river. They rested and bathed. Kontu and Watota wrestled in the water and Gunt ate periwinkles. Yovo seemed much rested and refreshed and he said, "We will cross the river while daylight lasts. Cut cane for a raft for our bundles and possessions."

Kontu was not pleased. Cutting cane was hard work. But they all helped and soon had many bunches of cane tied together with vines. They loaded the Sacred Packs and the spears and the skins onto this raft and the lot of them went into the water, shoving the raft before them. The current was not too swift and all of them but Yovo were strong swimmers. They soon had reached the far shore.

"This is a good camping place," Yovo said. "And certainly there is plenty of water. We will stay here for the night."

Kontu was pleased. There was still daylight, and he was feeling energetic after his bath. He decided suddenly to explore ahead a little bit, as he had to do in the days before the encounter with the Primitives. He followed the path in the twilight looking here and there for branches that might lead in the direction they wished to take tomorrow, looking for the tracks of game, simply looking. He heard someone behind him and whirled to see Neeka coming toward him.

"Did I frighten you, Little Brother?" she asked teasingly. But her voice was not unkind. She seemed to feel less bitterly toward Kontu now that she had Watota to sneer at. She caught up with him.

"You travel too far alone," she said. "The old one worries about you. He thinks you carry some of the load of his magic and help him out."

Kontu was pleased. He was pleased that Neeka would think such a thing, Yovo must have shown it in some way, and that pleased him too. "I am only going to the top of that ridge," he said, pointing.

They walked together up the hill. And then they stood in silence, for in the valley below them many men walked and sat and six small fires burned slowly.

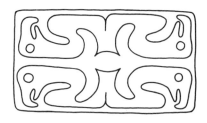

Chapter Eleven

The Adena went forward slowly into the circle of the fires; Yovo first, making the sign of peace, with Watota beside him, as the strongest and best suited to defend the old man, should need arise. Kontu followed, and Gunt and Neeka walked behind him.

In that shadowy place where the light of the fires met the darkness, they halted and Yovo called out, "Let us walk the white path together. Let us have peace between us."

Nearly all of the men swung toward them or turned their heads in that direction, more in surprise than real alarm. Several called out in laughing voices and finally one of them came forward and said in the language of the Adena, "We are traders, Grandfather. Not warriors. One of the goods we carry with us is peace, for no man strikes a fair bargain with a spear point."

Yovo nodded and the rest of the party crowded around him. Most of the traders paid them little heed but two or three came to stare curiously.

Kontu was relieved. He had assumed Neeka was right when she ran to tell Yovo that the fires in the valley ahead belonged to traders. He had wanted very much to join them. But he had been afraid. Suppose she was wrong?

He had not taken part in the argument that followed their return. Watota wanted to go by himself to spy on those who camped beyond the ridge. Yovo wished to wait until daylight, but Neeka wanted to go now. In the end Watota had agreed with the girl in urging them to go ahead.

Kontu knew why. They were all eager to see a group of traders with their wares. And it might be that one of the traders knew enough Adena words to tell them news of distant places or tales of their adventures. Even Yovo might hope for a clue concerning the Eye in the Forest. By daylight, who knew? The lot of them might have traveled on, scattered in every direction with their trade goods.

Kontu had heard about these markets, where traders from far regions gathered, sometimes to swap commodities or to report that the men of the North no longer wanted black whorled shells for ornaments, but preferred white ones; or that the people of the South valued pipes of a particular red stone from northern lands; or that ocher paint was in short supply. Who would not want to see such a gathering or hear such talk?

One of the traders pointed to the stamp on Yovo's forehead.

"A priest!" he exclaimed. "I know the mark. What is an Adena priest doing here?"

Yovo hesitated. "Our people are in trouble," he answered. "We are on a mission decreed by the gods."

The trader who had first spoken to them gestured toward Neeka. "She is no Adena," he said. "What is she doing with you? Did the spirits send her to show you the way?"

"She is a friendless wanderer," Yovo answered. He seemed ill at ease. Kontu had the notion that the old priest wished they had not joined the traders. "She is not a member of our mission. She travels toward her home and merely walks with us for company."

Well, that was true. Kontu wondered how long she

would go with them and whether, if they found the Eye, Yovo would ask her to leave them. It was a thing he had not thought of before.

"You are welcome to stay with us for company," said the trader. "My name is Itza which you might not remember, but you will not forget my face."

Indeed. No one would forget once they had seen the blue-black dots tattooed over his face. Even his ears had these marks. All the traders had some distinguishing symbol, something quickly and easily seen. They traveled among unfamiliar people and did not want to be mistaken for an enemy. But of them all, Itza's decorations were the best.

A few of the other traders who spoke the Adena language also told their names.

"You may sleep here," said Itza, pointing to one of the fires. "I will stay here for several days to await an old friend from west of the Great River, and you may be my guests." He smiled with a sudden glint of mischief and Kontu knew that being his guests meant helping him fetch firewood and kill game and skin and cook it. But he doubted any of his companions would mind.

It had been a hard day and all of them were glad to lie down and sleep, though Kontu could not resist sitting up once or twice when he awoke in the night to glance at all the low-burning fires and assure himself it was true—that he slept here among these men from every part of the land, all carrying their strange merchandise.

They were up early and Kontu made his morning ceremony hastily. Yovo looked at him reprovingly. But even Yovo was soon wandering among the traders, looking with wonder and delight at the bags full of shells, some creamy white, some banded with buff, small and delicate and just right for jewelry. There were thick sheets of mica and

· 80 ·

nuggets of copper and copper beaten into rings and bracelets. Among the Adena people copper and mica were sacred things, used for ceremonial objects, and Kontu was a little shocked to see that these copper rings and bracelets were evidently intended simply for adornment. There were bright feathers and black obsidian and colored pebbles and large shells, paints and dyes, furs and skins, a marvelous show.

Neeka and Kontu and Gunt walked back and forth inspecting all these beautiful things. Watota and Yovo were more aloof, but they too could not avoid touching the strange shiny obsidian and asking the use of various objects. Most of the goods were for jewelry or for the special needs of sacred ceremonies.

Gunt touched some spiraled shells with a thick finger. "Very handsome," he told Neeka and Kontu. He seemed to have something else to say and finally he said it. "But this morning near the river. I saw something more beautiful still. I saw a little fine spiderweb hung up in the air and all covered with dew. It sparkled in the sun. No chieftain could wear such a thing on his robe, but if he could. . . ." He made a gesture at the shells, as though they were so many dead leaves. Gunt was strange, Kontu thought again.

The traders strolled about inspecting what was offered and making bargains: So many lumps of graphite for a bag of salt, so much mica for so many medicinal beans. At midday they ate, much bartering having been completed and some of the traders preparing to go on their way. There was a feast of game and turkeys, late berries and herbs and roots, fish from the river and bigger, sweeter grapes than the Adena had ever seen or tasted. Kontu had not felt so happy for a long time.

The merchants who spoke the Adena language came to talk with Yovo and ask questions and tell tales. One of them wore a necklace of huge bear fangs and Watota could not take his eyes from it. At last he asked, "What kind of bear has teeth like that?"

"He who walks like a man and looks over mountains," answered the wearer. "In the western lands these bears live, and it is said they are too big and fierce to be killed. Whole towns have tried and failed, losing half their people in the struggle. But I have fangs and claws to trade, so some of the bears must die."

Another man spoke up. "I have been once to that place and I did not see the bears but I saw where their claws had shredded huge trees. I was glad not to meet one. But that is a land of strangeness and mystery, where water boils out of the earth in tall spouting fountains and then stops and comes again . . . where rivers run at the bottom of chasms so deep and steep no man or animal could escape from them."

A third man jeered, "Those are not marvels compared to the mountains I have seen far to the south. They smoke and breathe flames and throw themselves high in the air."

And still another said, "All those things are the work of the gods, who can do anything. They are astonishing, indeed. But always to my mind the things that ordinary men do are stranger. I know of a people who live in stone houses as high as the sky and who can make rivers run where they wish and stop when they wish."

The tales went on, but in quiet tones, for they told of hallowed spots where a man felt small and awestruck. Itza declared, "I have seen a place like these you speak of. To the south and east, a high plateau between two rushing rivers. Not too far from here. A place with great stone and earthen walls and a strange entranceway, a place that must have taken many generations of men to complete. I have been there twice and it is deserted, I have never seen a human being near it. But I do not venture far inside. It is a temple and the gods still dwell there and it makes me afraid. . . ."

Kontu almost cried out. Was this the Sacred Eye? He tried not to look at Yovo. But the priest showed no special interest in what Itza said. Instead he asked about paths leading away from this traders' marketplace, saying tomorrow they must be on their way. Itza answered and the group broke up.

The rest of the day Kontu and Neeka watched the traders packing their wares and sampled foods at the fires. Kontu had supposed Yovo would not allow them this day of rest and festivity, but the old man seemed in an odd mood and spent the afternoon sitting under a tree far from the camps, frowning and pondering. But he woke them very early the next morning and they set off with only the briefest good-byes to those traders who were stirring about.

They walked a well-traveled path at first, easy to follow. But after a day Yovo chose another trail, at a fork, and it was more troublesome. The leaves were falling and sometimes hid the way.

Yovo grumbled. "When the days are shorter, and the light less," he complained to no one in particular, "we should have a plain path."

Kontu was surprised. Was Yovo remonstrating with the gods? He would have scolded Kontu, or even any of the others, for saying such things. On a sacred mission one did not quarrel with what the spirits sent, one accepted it and went on. It was, Kontu thought, likely that the old man was simply provoked with himself, for he traveled very slowly; when they lost the way, he sat, hugging his knees and staring into space, while the others searched.

They traveled on for days and one midday Yovo stopped them and said simply that they had taken the wrong path. They must go back. And back they went.

They returned to the well-worn path and took it, heading south and a little bit eastward. Two days later, when a rain as sharp and fine as bone splinters beat against them they came to a man-made structure—earthen mounds and walls and a sort of entrance. It was a curious thing to come on in the forest, with no warning. Yovo did not comment but brought them to a halt. Under the shelter of a hemlock he built a fire, and with Kontu to help prayed and chanted and performed a ceremony Kontu had never seen before.

Was this what they were seeking? Was the Eye in the Forest inside this entryway? It did not look like the place Kontu had seen in his dream. He wanted to tell Yovo so but somehow did not dare.

He hated leaving the shelter of the hemlock and the friendly warmth of the little fire, but when Yovo left he followed obediently. The others waited under another of the thick dark trees.

"Stay," said Yovo. "Kontu will go with me through the doorway. We will return soon."

In the rain Kontu followed the old man between the mounds and through the long narrow entrance in the wall. Was this the place? He did not remember it this way, a young forest surrounded by an earthen wall. They rambled through the little new trees, this way and that.

Then they followed the wall for a space. Certainly the wall was like the one he had seen in his dream. But there could be many such walls in the forest across this broad land. From old sacred stories he knew that. And not so long ago this little young forest had been a smooth meadow.

And then suddenly Kontu saw something he did indeed recognize—a spring, a small deep pool, clear and full of bubbles and the reflections of the cloudy sky. He knew it right away, the little mysterious bright pool of his dream!

Chapter Twelve

"This is it!" Kontu gasped. "This is the place of my dream, Father Yovo! The pool . . . I saw it in my dream! Just as plainly as I see it now."

Yovo did not answer. He stared down into the spring for a long time and then moved off again, following the high wall of earth circling this sacred place, containing the holiness here on this flat ridgetop surrounded by flowing waters.

Kontu recognized it all now. He pointed out to Yovo how the hill had been sheared from this spot down to the river where he had searched in vain for a way up from the gorge. Farther along he found the tower of great trees marching up the side of the ridge, but Yovo seemed not to be interested. Beyond the trees Kontu stopped in amazement, for he was looking down on the way he had come up finally into the Eye, climbed up the slope through boulders and trees, with the frothy pools and river rapids to his right. It was all as he had dreamed, and he turned to Yovo.

"It was that way in the dream," Kontu said softly. "This is it, this is the Eye." And still there was no response from the priest.

The two of them walked all around the hilltop enclosure and back to the strange entrance. "Go tell the others to make a camp nearby," said Yovo at last. "Have your meal and I will come later." He stood still, fingering the medicine bag sewn to his shirt, and Kontu waited for him to say something more, but he did not.

Yovo was dismissing his assistant. Whatever he planned to do, he planned to do alone. Kontu was disappointed, he had thought, since he had had the dream which told them this was the Eye, that he would participate in Yovo's ceremonies here. He should be the one to smoke the Sacred Breath and wait for the spirits to speak. But no.

The rain had stopped, though the wind was damp and cold. Gunt had already built a cooking fire and supper was soon ready, for game had been plentiful of late and they carried much meat with them. Under the hemlock boughs, the air grew warm and smoky and they ate in contented silence. Only Kontu strained to hear the sound of Yovo's footsteps returning.

The fire burned down and he fed it sparingly, keeping the embers barely aglow. Gunt and Neeka stretched out and went to sleep, and Watota, who had been silent about his bear hunt since the traders' tales of huge ones in western lands, suddenly began once more to tell how he had crept forward with his spear and throwing stick, how he had followed silently up the hillside— Kontu sprang up.

"Yovo!" he cried.

The old man stared at him unseeingly. He staggered a little as he walked. Kontu seized him by the arm and helped him down beside the fire. The priest's flesh was as cold as death, and Kontu stirred up the ashes and threw on some sticks so the fire blazed. He drew Yovo's pallet near the flames.

"Here . . . here is a deer liver we saved you . . . eat," he urged, scraping the singed morsel from the warm stone onto a bark flake. Yovo ate a few bites and then thrust the liver and bark away from him and stretched out on his bed.

His eyes shut and he seemed asleep almost at once.

Watota reached across the fire and snatched up the liver. He quickly downed it. Then he began again his story of the bear hunt, and Kontu nodded awhile without hearing a word. What had happened inside the enclosure? Why had Yovo behaved so strangely? He turned away from Watota and lay down on his skins and went to sleep while Watota's voice still went on and on.

In the morning Yovo was gone. Kontu awoke first of the others and looked at once for the priest and saw that his place was empty. All day Kontu waited under the hemlock. It was sunny and warmer; the rest of them fetched firewood and slept and ate and squabbled, but Kontu merely sat, waiting. Yovo, he knew, was asking for a sign, that this was indeed the Eye in the Forest, the place that would restore the Adena people to health and good fortune.

The spirits must speak to the priest, not to his subordinate. So much Kontu now understood. But this was the place, he was certain this was the place, he had seen it in his dream. Why would the spirits guide them here, safeguarding them at every step, and give him the knowledge to recognize the Eye, yet withhold such knowledge from Yovo?

At sunset he could bear it no longer and walked to the entryway, only to find Yovo coming toward him. The old man seemed weary and frail but he did not have the strange tranced look he had had last night. Instead his eyes were full of sadness and doubt. The spirits had not broken their silence.

"I begin to believe this is not the place," he said slowly to Kontu as they met in the entranceway.

"But it is, Father," cried Kontu. "It is the place I saw in my dreams. Exactly the same!"

Yovo glanced at him swiftly. "Kontu, you are not yet

priest," he answered a little sharply. "The spirits may speak through you . . . and then again they may not. Or they may speak to deceive. Tell me once again about your dream. Tell me everything."

Kontu told, speaking carefully, remembering everything, trying to make Yovo believe. To himself, he sounded suddenly like Watota telling of the bear hunt. Yovo nodded, the way he nodded when Watota talked. With an effort, Kontu finished his story. He felt bewildered and discouraged.

"You see what that might mean," Yovo responded. "It might mean that we would come to this place and take it to be the Eye, and yet we would be wrong. And believing so, as we might have done, brought our people to an even worse pass than that which they face now."

He walked on toward the camp. Kontu watched him go. In the dusk, in the long shadows of the walls and the trees, he stood for a moment hearing the crickets in the weeds. Slowly he passed into the gateway and down the long dim hall and out into the walled enclosure. The light was fading but it was easy to find the pool. He stood looking down, the little bubbles floated up through the reflection of the bright evening sky. And suddenly the water darkened, scum drifted over the reflection, the sky itself grew livid and bruised and hideous. Kontu turned and ran.

Chapter Thirteen

Gunt groaned as Yovo worked over his swollen foot. White poison oozed from the wound. Kontu watched in horrified fascination. He did not like to see Gunt suffer, but he could not take his eyes from the sight. Besides, as priest he must one day treat such illnesses himself.

Gunt had stepped on a sharply-broken piece of cane as he helped Watota search for his spear in a marshy place along the smaller of the two rivers. It had not seemed a bad hurt, no one had paid too much attention to it. They were all busy preparing to leave the place and go on searching for the Sacred Eye.

Yovo had spent many hours in prayer; he had thrown the ancient and holy bones of Father Eagle onto his deerskin painted to show the four corners of the earth. Soon, very soon, Father Eagle would speak to him and show him the way to go, and they would travel on. They must be ready to leave at once, for time was growing short, with winter almost upon them.

And then Gunt had awakened with his foot puffy and the stab red and running. It was plain he could not walk with such a sore.

Yovo was worried; he had to go on with all his prayers for guidance and at the same time he had to perform healing ceremonies for Gunt.

"I will stay here and follow when my foot is better," Gunt explained to anyone who would listen.

But it was no matter, for Father Eagle had not yet spoken, or at any rate not spoken in a way that could be understood. It was a trying time and they were all tense. Poor Gunt lay staring into the fire for hours and his ankle swelled more with each day. This morning it was even worse, and his moans made Kontu almost sick with pity and soon he got up and walked away.

He would not be missed, he thought bitterly. Yovo never asked for his help anymore. The initiate who had brought them to this place was given no part in the rituals and not allowed to witness the throwing of the ancient bones.

The day was bright and crisp, the leaves of the beeches reflected the sun in a red glow, the winds blew milkweed down and the seeds of grasses along the earth. There was a little icy edge to the wind, the breath of winter. It was too late to travel on, and they all knew it, no matter what Father Eagle said. Kontu splashed across the river, where the rocks made a fording place, and glanced back at the strange high walls of the sacred place. How many men and women must have worked over long years to build this temple. People of great holiness must have dedicated their lives to it, such a people as the Adena.

He walked on, scuffling a little through the leaves and pondering as he went. If this was not the Eye for which they searched, why had he been given his uncanny dream? Why had they been brought to this temple? For temple it surely was. And now why were they being forced to stay? Was it chance? Or some evil-wisher?

Or was it because Kontu was not fit to be a priest. Had he not dropped the Sacred Fire? Had he not insulted Fire, so that Fire had misled them and brought them to a place that had the outward look of the Eye of the Adena, but not the inward spirit? Perhaps that was why Yovo had received no sign and why he no longer wanted Kontu to take part in the rituals and ceremonies. He had begun to doubt his helper and had cast him aside, for he was not a true helper but a hindrance.

Sorrow like a fist closed over Kontu's heart. He wished suddenly that Neeka was with him. She had gone alone out of the camp earlier in the day. But often of late they had walked the woods together and sometimes she had let him use her spear, not caring that he was awkward with it. She was his real friend.

He came on some withered persimmons and ate them. A bear had been there before him and left him only a handful. A few steps away the bear had split open a rotten stump in search of beetles and grubs. The marks looked recent; Kontu went forward more quietly and cautiously. He was not eager to meet a bear. He had no weapon, and perhaps Father Eagle would see fit to get rid of this bad student priest by letting a bear devour him.

Something moved ahead of him and Kontu stopped still, fearful of a bear. It was not a bear, but an old woman.

Kontu was afraid and surprised. He and the others had not known there was a village near them. The area had seemed empty of inhabitants and since all the Adena had felt the weight of the hands of the spirits in this place, its ancient quiet and holiness, they had supposed that everyone felt it also, that everyone considered it too hallowed to occupy. The Adena people had never built towns close to their shrines, but always at a distance, sometimes a considerable distance.

Now Kontu knew there must be a village close by, for here was an old woman, bending and scrabbling for acorns to fill her basket. She would not be far from home. He watched her as she bobbed along, stumbling occasionally as she searched.

At last she seemed satisfied and swung the basket to her shoulder. Kontu followed, keeping hidden, which was not a difficult thing to do for she was unsuspicious, bent under her basket of nuts. He knew when they were approaching the town for he could hear voices and there was a faint smell of fire and of cooking meat.

He hid in the laurel bushes on a hillside and watched. It was not a village. It was a camp, scarcely more sturdy or permanent than the one Kontu and the others were occupying. A hut, hastily constructed and looking ready to fall in a good wind, some racks where roots were drying, a cooking hearth—that was all.

The old woman carried her basket to a big storage pit and dumped the acorns in. Then she went to the hearth, where a pot sat in hot ashes, and stirred the stew with a stick and helped herself to a bowlful. Another woman was taking nuts out of a second storage pit and putting them into a huge reed basket, and Kontu saw a third pit beyond that.

A girl came out of the rough hut and stirred the stew again. And then Kontu saw two men approaching through the woods. They were dressed in skins wrapped loosely around their waists, and they carried no weapons. He was relieved to notice that.

When the girl saw them she dropped the stick by the pot and ran eagerly to meet them. One of the men greeted her affectionately, but the other brushed on by and went straight to the great basket full of nuts from the pit and strapped it carefully to his back. He shouted at the other man, who laughed and shouted back, then went to fetch another of the big baskets. The two of them set off again the way they had come and the girl ran after them, calling something to them. The man who had treated her so lovingly must be her father and she must be entreating him to stay, Kontu decided. When she came back to the fire she looked unhappy.

Kontu waited for something else to happen, but nothing did, only a third woman appeared with two children even younger than the girl. Evidently they had been gathering more acorns, for they carried baskets which they emptied into the pits.

By and by Kontu remembered his own encampment and that he should warn Yovo and the others. As quietly as he was able, he slipped through the shining leaves of the laurel and made his way back across the river. Gunt was sleeping by the fire, Watota was plucking a turkey. Neeka knelt by Yovo, speaking to him softly. Kontu came up to them and interrupted.

"Father Yovo," he said urgently, "we are in danger. There are people living near."

Yovo did not look at him. "Yes, Neeka has seen them and told me about them," he answered evenly. Kontu frowned. He had failed at even this simple task, bringing the news of the strangers and their threat.

Neeka spoke to him as much as to Yovo. "They are not living here," she assured them. "They are Nut Gatherers, who follow the harvests from place to place. They do not have any place where they all live together, but only these stations where the women live and gather the nuts and care for themselves and the children. The men live elsewhere and hunt for meat and bring it to the women when they come for the baskets of nuts, for food, for they are not very good hunters."

"They mean us no harm and we will stay out of their way," said Yovo. "They would not venture here, I believe. And we cannot move till Gunt improves."

Gunt, as if hearing his name spoken, stirred and moaned in his dream of fever.

Neeka said, "He needs a good broth. Marrowbone soup, that would help clear the poison from his head."

Yovo answered, "Yes, that would certainly help. But we have no pot big enough for stewing marrowbones and we have no marrowbones."

Watota put in quickly, "I will kill an elk. My spear misses nothing these days."

"The bowl that carries the Sacred Fire would do very well," said Neeka casually.

There was a horrified silence. "Daughter, you speak in ignorance," reproved Yovo at last. His lips were tight with shock. Kontu himself felt as if someone had struck him sharply.

"What would we do with the Sacred Fire?" he wondered aloud. "Would we dump it on the ground? Fire would never be our friend again!"

Look how he had brought trouble to them all by dropping some of the Sacred Fire in the house of the Primitives' chief, he wanted to add, but he did not.

Neeka pointed to the little fire that blazed among them. "Is that not Fire? Did it not come from the Sacred Bowl? Is it not dumped on the ground?" She did not wait for an answer but spun on her heel and walked away.

The others stared after her. "It is not the same thing," said Yovo uncomfortably. "The little flames that Sacred Fire spits out to cook our meat, that is not the same thing." The priest turned to Kontu. "She is not to blame that she does not know or understand the ways of the spirits." Kontu nodded, thinking Yovo would never defend him as he always did Neeka when she erred. But then she had not been selected to be a future priest.

Watota went back to plucking the turkey; Kontu stared

after Neeka; Yovo went on watching Gunt. But the air around the little fire was troubled and uneasy.

Neeka was back before the evening meal to tell what she had learned. Again the next day she reported on the activities of the Nut Gatherers. They were getting ready to leave, they had scoured the woods of nuts; the men had come for the last basketful. The old woman Kontu had followed had died in the night, had simply not waked from her sleep, and they had buried her in an empty storage pit.

"They did not mourn her long," Neeka related. "They sang a dirge and then they dumped her in the empty storage pit with a few odds and ends and kicked some dirt over her. . . ."

Once again the Adena men stared at her in shock and fascination. How could she watch the burial rites of another people? And how could those other people treat their dead so meanly? Even Gunt, who seemed somewhat better, gasped a little, listening.

But by nightfall he was worse, moaning and sighing on his pallet. Yovo applied hot poultices made of herbs and lichen to his wound every few minutes, snatching one off and slapping on another, till Gunt groaned more than ever, then at last fell into a fitful sleep. In the morning his mind wandered.

Kontu wished Yovo had not forbade him to go with Neeka today. He did not like staying here and hearing Gunt. Watota did not seem to be bothered. He had killed a deer and he went on talking about his prowess and how he had thrown his spear cleanly and triumphantly.

It was right for a huntsman to boast about his prey and to tell of his cunning. Kontu had heard such talk all his life, had even enjoyed it, and had been proud when it was his father or one of his uncles rejoicing over a kill. But hearing

Watota often irritated him. Did he envy the older boy, he wondered? He had never killed more than a slow-trundling opossum himself. He was no hunter, and now it seemed he was no priest. He had cause to envy Watota.

He heard the sound of running footsteps and looked up. Neeka hurried toward them.

"They have gone, as I said they would," she cried. "And see what they have left behind." She held up a good-sized pot. "It will hold many marrowbones to make Gunt well." She turned it around. "It has a hole, here in the side, but it can be easily mended. . . ."

Yovo uttered a scream of terror. He flung himself between Neeka and Gunt. "Take it away!" he shouted. "Take it away! It has been killed, the pot has been killed! Take it away!"

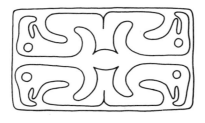

Chapter Fourteen

For a moment they were all crying out, in anger and terror, Gunt in his fever and Watota in ignorance and fear, and Yovo and Kontu in prayer against wickedness. Together the priest and his initiate chanted a formula against great ill which had come to them both at once, and for that moment Kontu felt strong and a priest again.

But the angry voice of Neeka rose above all the others. She seized Yovo by the shoulder and her voice pierced the air like a spear blade.

"Old man!" she shouted. And he ceased his prayer and stared at her. Kontu stared too. He had not seen her ever look so enraged.

She pushed the old priest roughly, and Kontu feared for him.

"Listen, old man," she screamed. "Did you think I dug up the dead woman and stole one of her pots? Did you think I would need do such a thing? Did you think I was so stupid as to think you would take such a pot?" She was trembling and pale.

The rest of them fell into stupefied silence. Neeka's voice shook but she went on more calmly. "I found the pot, old man, in their camp after the Nut Gatherers left. They dropped it and made a hole and did not think it worth their while to take it with them. I thought it worth my while. The pots that went into the pit with the old woman are still there. I took nothing from a grave—nothing."

She glared around at them all and then turned her face back to Yovo. "You have been good to me, Grandfather, and I have been good to you. I have not set a foot inside this sacred place for fear of offending you. I do not believe in your gods. I do not believe that a pot can go into the next world with a dead person. I do not believe that a pot has a spirit or that you can let it out to travel by making a little hole in its side. But you believe that and I would not mock your belief."

Kontu was amazed at her. She had more courage than any of them, he thought. She was alone and the gods must hate her and yet she was never afraid. Even Yovo must respect such courage. The old priest did indeed look a little shamed.

"I am going now." Neeka went on. "I will take my spear and my pot and go my way. I will remember that you were kind to me once, old man."

Yovo put a hand on her arm. Kontu remembered the scars of cuts and burns now hidden by her skin shirt. "Wait, Daughter," he begged. "I was wrong. I did not understand about the pot. Stay with us and forgive my stupidity. I am an old man and much troubled. It is too late for us to travel; there is snow coming very soon. Father Eagle does not speak, neither Fire nor Snake gives us direction. A priest may pray and study and be holy all his life and yet not always know what the spirits wish of him. But there was a sign from them that you should travel with us, that . . . that I remember."

He looked a long time at Neeka. "Stay with us," he said, and his voice begged, said silently, Stay with us because we need and want you, not because the gods command it.

Kontu watched her closely and saw something soften the harsh and sullen lines of her face. She did not answer but went over and lay down on her pallet, and they all knew that she would stay. And he wondered if Yovo had done the right thing.

The next day Neeka made a broth in her mended pot and they all had some of it, most of it going to Gunt. Kontu was past caring whether the pot was a pot which had been ceremonially killed to release its spirit into the world of the dead. He was willing to take almost any risk to keep peace among them. The broth was good and he drank it and even Yovo had a reluctant mouthful.

Yovo worked day and night with Gunt. He sprayed dark powder from puff balls on the warrior's foot. He placed hot stones along both sides of the swollen leg and threw water on them to make steam, covering all with a deerskin to sweat the sickness away. One night Kontu could see Gunt was better, his fever gone and the swelling subsiding. Still Yovo ministered to him—teas from various herbs, which he made Gunt drink, one different tea after another until Kontu was sure the warrior would slosh away down the gorge.

Three days later Gunt stood up on wobbly legs, and who could say whether Neeka's soup or Yovo's medicines and prayers had made him well?

"Now, Yovo," Gunt said, "you may travel on and I will follow when I am stronger."

"Yes," answered the old man vaguely. He had seemed to shrink and shrivel in the last few days. Gunt's healing had taken a great deal out of him. He looked very old and very weary. He made no move to leave—and they all knew it was too late. Yovo lay on his pallet and slept and did not perform the rites of a priest or tell the others what to do.

At last Watota said, "He will die soon." He glanced at

Kontu. "Then there will be only you to tell us what to do, little half-priest. We will all die, running around in this strange land with nothing to guide us but your crooked little rabbit track of wisdom."

Kontu said nothing in reply. There was nothing he could say. He did not know enough to guide them, it was true. His one adventure into real magic had brought them here and now it had all fallen into a kind of madness, as though the spirits had scorned him.

He waited, day after long day, for Yovo to get better. He did not himself neglect his sacred rituals and duties; he awoke before light and went to bathe in the icy river and say his prayers. Every day he went inside the walled circle and prayed and sang. Once he had crept up to the little pool and looked in, remembering his terrible dream and expecting it to happen again, but nothing happened, the bubbles rose in the water and he saw faintly reflected the bare branches of a little tree to one side. And then he crept away again.

Neeka was impatient with them all and squabbled continually and sharply with Watota. She tried to make Yovo eat, shaking him out of his sleep and forcing him to swallow some special tidbit.

"He has fasted until he is only bone," she said. "There is plenty to eat, he must eat."

"Yes, he must eat and stay alive," Watota threatened. "For when he dies, you go."

"Should we build a hut?" asked Gunt hastily, for he changed the subject whenever they quarreled.

"Feed the old man and he will grow strong and give you an answer," said Neeka tartly.

"Let the little half-priest tell us," snarled Watota. "With his one eye and his one hand and his one foot, let him tell us."

Kontu grew angrier and angrier. He was angry at Neeka because she was right, Yovo should not be allowed to sleep himself to death. He was angry at Gunt for being nothing. He was angriest at Watota. Kontu knew he could not help it that he had not yet learned how to be a priest, yet Watota's taunts aroused all his fears, made him doubt more than ever that he would be a real sorcerer. Nevertheless he knew more of magic than the others. If Father Yovo died, Kontu would have to do what he could to lead the others and show them what was right—it was the duty of a priest, even a half-priest. And there was no one else to do it.

It did not snow in spite of Yovo's prediction. Instead it rained, an icy-cold steady downpour that filtered down through the hemlocks and made the fire sputter and drenched the beds.

"Shall we build a hut?" asked Gunt again, after two days without a letup in the deluge. Watota looked at Kontu. "Shall we build a hut?" he repeated derisively. Kontu met his eyes and answered suddenly.

"No, it is too late and the work is too hard . . . we will make a better shelter here, under the hemlocks. We will start now."

So they did, making a roof of cane bundles and sheets of bark laid across the limbs overhead, and walls of more cane held secure by vines. It kept out the rain and most of the wind. They were comfortable if the wind did not blow too hard down the river gorge, swaying the hemlocks.

The Nut Gatherers, thought Kontu, must live a life scarcely better than this, between travels to spots where they could forage. It made a sad contrast to the neat sturdy houses of the Adena, who lived in pretty villages with the dwellings widely spaced so that each family had fields where they raised their own food. They hunted only occasionally for skins or for meat. Kontu supposed the Nut

Gatherers' life was a way that suited them, and yet it must be hard to be a *people*, with no place that belonged to them and no place where they might all live together. One might as well be a beetle or a moth.

It was going to be hard for the five of them to be a people too, he thought. So small a group, yet with Yovo very nearly the same as dead and the presence of Neeka to worry Kontu and irk Watota, it would be hard to band together and act as one. But they must. The months of cold and perhaps hunger that lay ahead of them meant they must cooperate and live in harmony or perish.

It was up to him, he knew in the furthest corner of his mind, it was really up to him to make them be a people, not beetles scurrying aimlessly about. Some way, he must do it.

During the first weeks he thought he could not do it. Yovo grew stronger and soon was up and about. But he often did not seem to know where he was or why he was there. It was frightening. He wandered about looking for his house and his wife and asking why none of his friends came to see him.

"We are not at home, Father Yovo," Kontu explained over and over. "We have traveled a long way to look for the Eye in the Forest."

"Ah, yes," Yovo would answer and his eyes would clear and he might even spend an afternoon praying and consulting all the objects in his small medicine bag. But then he would forget and ask plaintively once more why they did not return to their dwellings. They all had to watch him carefully to be sure that he did not leave the camp and get lost or fall into the river. He seemed worse when the weather was very cold, but fortunately he slept long and heavily at such times.

One thing they were spared was snow; it scarcely snowed at all, though in the mornings often the powdery frost was as thick as snow. It was a different winter from the winters the Adena people had experienced far to the north. The cold was often intense but lasted only a few days, followed by icy pouring rain, rain and rain and rain, so that the hemlocks drooped and the river rose and roared and swirled close to their shelter.

Watota would have preferred snow. Who could hunt in such weather? He seldom saw a deer, never an elk. Gunt and Neeka wove a fishnet from plant stems and long flexible roots and they ate fish often; but many days they had to be content with their old diet of snails and beetles or the inner bark of trees pounded and cooked with fish bones.

Actually, these days made Kontu happier. Hunger drew them together somehow. Watota made life less miserable for them all when he had nothing to boast about. Neeka made them give the best of everything to Yovo; they all felt it was the right thing to do, and sacrificing the goose liver or the last of the deer stew to the priest, with prayers to heal him, made him seem indeed a priest and man of power.

Kontu consoled himself; half-priest or not, he served a man who was a true magician, to whom the spirits spoke.

The days wore on and food became harder and harder to obtain. Kontu worried, for he did not know many hunting prayers or rites. He knew more about weather ceremonies, as Yovo did. Every day he asked Water to go back into the river. Every day he asked Fire to make the sun shine. And it happened. The rain stopped, the sun came out.

Gunt and Neeka caught more fish. Neeka found a huge turtle. But Watota, though he saw many deer tracks in the wet earth, glimpsed only a few of the animals themselves and they escaped his spear.

"It is the girl," the young warrior muttered at last and

Kontu answered shortly, "Perhaps it is. But it must be that the spirits wish it to be so, for Tobacco and Fire, Snake and Eagle, have not spoken to say she should leave. Yovo has said she was meant to stay with us and he has had a sign."

Watota hesitated. "What do you say?" he asked at length.

Kontu stared at him. "What difference does it make?" he replied. "I am only a half-priest."

"The old one is nearly dead," Watota said. "Perhaps he cannot find the strength to send her away. Perhaps Tobacco will tell you to do so."

Kontu knew what Watota was doing. He was stunned that the warrior would want him to pretend that he had had a message he could not possibly have received. Watota must have seen the anger and shock in Kontu's face. He dropped his eyes, ashamed.

"I will be glad when the winter is over," was all he said. Kontu knew he meant much more. By spring Yovo would be dead and they would be on their way back to the villages of the Adena and Neeka could be left behind.

The next day it rained again. By the sputtering fire Gunt and Watota quarreled fiercely over the tough skin of a gar, unexpectedly caught in their net. Each claimed a greater need for the abrasive hide useful for polishing. Watota sprang to his feet, looking as though he would strike the older man. Kontu spoke suddenly and with a steadiness he scarcely felt, "Are we not all brothers? Let there be peace in this place. I will take the skin. Yovo will make better use of it."

Watota still stood, but Gunt smiled. "You are right, Kontu. This is too small a house for quarreling. Yovo should have the skin."

Watota after a moment relaxed.

Kontu prayed over and over, and finally it snowed, a

thin crisp snow good for hunting. He was pleased and stood looking out of the shelter over the white landscape.

Watota came and lingered beside him. "I will hunt," he said reluctantly. "Can you help my spear? Can you?"

Kontu kept his face impassive. He took the spear and the throwing stick gently in his hands and went to the fire. He held them in the fragrant smoke and prayed the hunting prayer he knew best.

He took from the Sacred Pack four stones, one red, three black, and repeating his prayer threw them into the air. The red stone rolled toward the west. "That way," he told Watota. "Hunt in that direction."

He rubbed the ashes from the fire on Watota's arms and forehead. He prayed.

In the afternoon Watota came home with a deer.

In the days that followed Kontu began to hope. There was less rain, Neeka and Watota both brought home game on occasion. They would live the winter through at any rate.

Spring came sooner in this place than in their own land. The sun died and then began his journey north, and in less than two moons the maple buds had begun to open and under the leaves on the forest floor the small pale fingers of plants began to push through the earth. Kontu found it hard to believe. It would still be many days till warm weather and new life of the world, but far fewer than for those back in the country of the Adena.

Now Kontu worried about Yovo more than ever. The old priest was awake most of the daylight hours, but he grew feebler. He never seemed to know where he was or why he was there. He did not recognize Gunt or even Kontu. Neeka he confused with his real daughter. And Watota he simply ignored.

Kontu was almost split open with anxiety and fear. With

warm weather all sorts of decisions must be made. And in the spring moon there was much for a priest to do, for priests help the new year to its birth and assure much game and a good harvest. Kontu was afraid. Something desperate must be done. He knew healing prayers and rituals and had assisted Yovo with many of them. But how presumptuous of him to act by himself as a healer, he who knew so little and had no sign of any sort that the spirits had chosen him, only the mockery of a vision of a dream of a ghost of a place, a place no one could yet claim was the Eye.

Still he must do something. One morning he opened the Sacred Pack and took out the Fire Bowl and the little packet of tobacco. So little. Dared he use it? His fingers trembled as he laid it aside, got out the rattles and tied them to his legs, and took the pot of paint to color his face.

Yovo stirred. He turned on his pallet and opened his eyes. The sight of the rattles and the Fire Bowl and the pipe seemed to waken him in fact. For the first time in a long while he appeared to see Kontu clearly. He almost smiled.

"No, no," he whispered. "Put them back. Bring me my own pipe and I will smoke a little, then I will eat."

When he had eaten, he dropped off to sleep again. But in a short while he sat up, looking stronger and refreshed. Two days later he was walking about. He was making ready to perform the Rituals of Spring, and Kontu waited to be asked to take part.

The old man seemed to be pottering about. It would take a long time for him to prepare all things and for him to receive a sign one way or another that Kontu might participate. Kontu could not endure it.

Kontu left the camp, where only Gunt squatted by the fire and Yovo sat singing softly on his blankets. Neeka and Watota were hunting, going off in opposite directions.

Kontu walked a long time, seeing on every hand the signs that spring was coming, in spite of the ice along the streams and the hoar shining in the hollows. He held in his hand the azalea buds swollen half again as big as his thumb, uncovered violets blooming in a sheltered spot, and saw a long string of ducks making their way north. He stared up at them and when he lowered his eyes, he jumped and cried out in fear at the strange speckled face he saw rising before him out of the bushes.

And then, "Itza!" he shouted. "Itza! Why are you here?"

Chapter Fifteen

Kontu took a step toward the trader. "Itza, I am Kontu," he said. "Do you remember me?"

Itza looked at him gravely for a little and then smiled. "The winter has changed you, Kontu," he replied at last. "You have grown bigger and you have grown older, much older."

Kontu was surprised. Yet it was true that his shirt was too small for him. He must have grown. As for being older, he was a winter older, but no wiser. He had learned little, during these months, of the things that a priest should know. Only how to be lonely and frightened and troubled, a long way from home with a great burden to carry. But now he was pleased and happy to see Itza.

"What are you doing here?" asked Itza. "Is this the ancient sacred place for which you were looking when we met?"

Kontu hesitated. "No, this is not the place," he answered slowly. And then quickly, "What are *you* doing here? There is no one to trade with here."

Itza glanced around as if half-expecting to see a village full of people eager to have his wares. Then he shook his head. "I came to see the great walled circle on the hilltop and the little spring that pictures the sky on its surface," he explained. "It is a place of very strong gods, I can feel them even here away from the Sacred Circle. A trader needs the help of all spirits, in whatever part of the earth he travels. When I can, I visit such places as this and ask the aid and protection of the deities who live there. I wish to offend no spirit, for I believe and trust in them all."

He laughed. "And that is why I am such a successful trader."

Kontu was shocked. The gods of the Adena people would never look after another people. But perhaps a trader, leading a solitary and wandering life, was different. And then he saw that Itza was not so solitary after all, for another man stood a short way behind him in the undergrowth. The second man carried on his back a pack bigger than Itza's.

"Is that another trader?" Kontu wanted to know. "He is not one of those we saw with you before."

Itza grinned and the tattooed dots around his mouth danced and leaped about in a fascinating way. "No, that is my helper," he answered. "I am such a successful trader that I have got someone to help me carry my wares."

He gestured to the other man. "He does not hear very well and does not speak, something is wrong with his throat or tongue. But he has a strong back and a willing heart. When I speak he listens and never argues with what I say."

The helper smiled and nodded at Kontu. "Have you a dwelling place near here? We will rest a few days," said Itza. "We would be glad of your company."

"And we of yours," Kontu answered politely.

He led the way to camp. Watota was there. He had killed some rabbits and he and Gunt were skinning them for cooking. The fire was warm, and Itza and his helper were made welcome; Yovo brewed a special tea to give strength to travelers and handed them a small bowl, saying, "Let us walk the same white path, Itza. Peace."

The trader thanked him and drank. Then he undid his packs, to show his wares. "The young woman you had with you," he said casually, "what has become of her? Did she die? Did you sell her to a slave trader?"

"She is with us still," Yovo answered in a mildly reproving voice. "She is gone but she will shortly be back. She is—hunting."

Itza did not comment. Was it out of courtesy for their feelings, Kontu wondered? Or did Itza in his travels often meet women who, like Neeka, could use a spear and support themselves the way most women could not?

After a moment Itza merely said, "She should see my goods. I have never had such things to trade."

It was so. There were marvels inside the skin packs. Feathers, such beautiful feathers.

"We had a great storm at my home near the sea," Itza said. "Many birds were killed and left lying on the sand. See these feathers, scarlet and pink. And these tiny birds with long bills and bright colors, I have never seen them before, but there were many of them. Great trouble to skin but well worth it, see how they gleam! And shells were washed up in vast numbers, different shells, shells I had not known existed. Look at these, and these. And here, look at this."

He held up a piece of a great conch shell, bigger than Kontu's two hands, white and gently curved. A mask, with two eye holes encircled with deep lines and scratches at the top to represent hair.

"Oh, a very fine mask," exclaimed Yovo. There was a tinge of regret in his voice. He had nothing to trade for such a mask, one that would hide a magician well, so that the gods would not hesitate to speak plainly through him.

Itza laughed a little. "It is not a mask, it is a pendant," he explained. "A thong goes through the holes and it hangs around one's neck."

Kontu picked it up. It would make a better mask, he thought. He held it to his face and the holes were exactly right for his eyes. Through the holes he saw Neeka coming toward the camp. She swung her spear, but she brought nothing else.

Watota jeered. "Have you left your dead elk behind?" he called out. "Surely you are strong enough to carry an elk back to camp over your shoulders!" She did not answer, instead she came forward and greeted Itza and began to look at all the treasures spread on the ground.

Watota picked up the ornaments, the ear plugs, and lip pins, but he was more fascinated by the black triangular teeth of some great sea fish, huge beyond imagining. With his thick fingers Gunt stroked the tiny bright bird skins and cradled the milky smooth river pearls in his palm. "What would you like to get in trade for these things?" he asked, and Itza answered, "Copper. There is great demand for copper south of here."

"What is this?" asked Neeka. She held up what looked like a small spear, with feathers at the tail. Itza was eager to tell.

"Oh, it is an arrow," he cried. "I meant to show it right away."

"What is an arrow?" Yovo was curious. He took the thing from Neeka's hand and remarked, "It looks like some priest's rod."

"No, it is a weapon," answered Itza. "Very good, much better than a spear. It is shot from a bow, but alas, I have lost my bow and do not know how to make a new one. A bow is hard to make, the wood must be strong and flexible and properly seasoned in the sun and the smoke of a fire. It is flat and narrow and long, with notches at each end, and a leather thong is slipped into the notches so that the bow bends and holds the thong taut. Then you fit the notch in the arrow's feathered end against the string, pull arrow and thong back, and aim the point across your fist so. . . ."

With quick movements of his hands he demonstrated, holding the feathers against his cheek and miming the presence of the bending bow. "Release the arrow and thong and the arrow leaps through the air, farther and faster and harder than a spear. The warrior who showed it to me was traveling through our village from the direction of the setting sun. He and his followers say that a bow and arrow are much better than a spear and throwing stick."

Itza shrugged. "I am not a fighter or hunter. I do not know, but they demonstrated it to me and I was amazed. I have no doubt but the bow and arrow will soon be in everyone's hands as the strangers told me."

"Warriors will say anything," said Watota scornfully. "I will keep my spear and leave such toys to those who do not know better."

"Oh, I would like to try it," Neeka exclaimed and Watota said contemptuously, "No doubt. It seems a weapon fit only for women."

He got up and walked away and Itza stared after him.

"It is supposed to be a very good weapon," he remarked at last. "If new and unusual."

"A spear and throwing stick have always been good enough for the Adena people," Yovo returned rather sharply. "There is no need to change."

Itza nodded and began to gather up his merchandise.

Yovo turned to Kontu. "Fire must cleanse you before you help in the Ritual of Spring," he said in a low voice. "Come, get ready for the ceremony."

Chapter Sixteen

The spring weather warmed; every day new greenery and flowers appeared, overhead and underfoot. Yovo was his old self, it seemed, and Watota and Neeka ignored each other rather than exchanging bitter words. Gunt spent long hours on the banks of the little rivers, staring down into the swirling water and enjoying the sunshine. It was a good and happy time and Kontu felt at peace and contented and thought of nothing but their happiness, and the spring rain and sun, and the strange and laughable stories Itza told.

And ever present in his soul was the glad knowledge that Fire had not been displeased with him. True, this place might not be the Eye in the Forest, as Kontu had hoped. But surely he had not been thrown aside, discarded by the spirits.

Then Itza spoke of traveling on, else he would miss the other traders. Yet he stayed, as if waiting, and this puzzled Kontu. Yovo also began to talk of leaving but he too seemed reluctant. Kontu understood that. The winter had been hard on Yovo, traveling had not been easy for him. He did however throw the sacred bones on the skin painted with the four quarters of the earth circle and determine that the Adena must head south.

Yet each bright and spicy sunrise with bird songs

showering down from the treetops found them all still together. Worries began to crowd into Kontu's mind, bigger and darker for having been away these last few days. And one morning he went inside the walls of the temple once more.

The grass was growing green and lush, and wild plum and Juneberry bloomed, and little new gold and pink leaves decorated some of the trees. He walked slowly around the walls and then made his way down the rocky path which he had first climbed up in his dreams. In his dreams? Such a lovely place. If this was not the Adena people's holy place, it should have been.

At the bottom of the cliffs ferns and flowers grew everywhere, in every crevice and cranny, and up and down the further hillsides, sheets of white and pink and blue and yellow flowers. He heard someone coming, and he turned to find Neeka walking along gazing down at the ground so that she did not see him. He called out and she looked up and smiled.

"I never saw a place like this," she said as she came toward him. "Spring is always beautiful, but this is like one of Itza's tales, I can scarcely believe it, even though it is here before my eyes."

Kontu's face darkened. "Itza will be leaving," he said. "I hate to see him go. We will miss him." Then he added, "And we will be going also for Yovo says we must travel south. I hate to leave this place."

"I do not mind leaving," Neeka said. "But I will miss you, Little Brother."

Kontu stared. "You mean, you are not traveling with us . . . you are going with him!" He was astonished. Neeka laughed.

"Why not?" she asked. "He travels toward my old home. He sees many strange and marvelous things. Every day is different with him, and he likes things that way."

She glanced at Kontu. "And I like things that way too."

Kontu nodded. He could not tell her how much he would miss her. But he would, he knew it with all his heart. He hated to think of the days ahead without Neeka.

"Did you really suppose that I would go on forever helping you find what you seek?" The old mocking scornful note was back in her voice. "It is too late for that. The cuts on my arms have healed but the scars are there, and on my heart are scars. No one will ever again tell me what to do. I will live in a hollow tree and hunt my own food, or I will die with my own spear through my throat, before I will live as others live."

Kontu looked down at the tiny star-shaped flower growing on the rock at the water's edge and knew she was right. She would be well-suited to the life of a trader. A woman who hunted and killed might very well become a trader and wander at her will. He had never heard of such a thing, but then there were many things he had not seen or heard of in his life till now.

"I see," he said. "Yes . . . yes, it is right for you to go. But I will miss you far more than I will Itza."

"The others will not miss me," she said without rancor.

"Yovo will," protested Kontu. "Your decision might send him back to his bed, sick beyond curing. He needs you."

"Not him," she answered. "He has a pupil to train and people to pray over and to look after—and a place to rededicate."

"This place?" gasped Kontu. "This is not the place we seek. This is not the Eye in the Forest."

"Yes, it is," she insisted. "Did you not have a dream? Did you not find this place in your inner world of magic?"

"You do not believe in magic," Kontu pointed out.

"No, but I believe in priests," she said quickly. "I have seen many peoples who would crumble into bits without their priests. I have watched you during the winter, Little Brother, and I saw how you held us all together. You are a priest and the old one knows it and is proud of you, though he does not say it. He knows too that this is the place, and that is why he has lain sick all winter and would not open his eyes. He feared that the spirits had favored you above him, a little, and he did not know why they would not speak to him. But perhaps they had their purposes."

"But he is leading us away," exclaimed Kontu.

"He has not left yet, has he?" pointed out Neeka. "He waits, hoping for a miracle."

Kontu thought a moment. "How did you know I had a dream?" he asked at last.

"I listened," she answered shortly. "Things you said and Yovo said and mutterings in the old man's sleep. One who lives as I have lived learns to listen."

Again he was quiet and heard from far away the sounds of geese honking across the sky. "I had a dream," he responded. "In my dream I saw this place, this very place. . . . I walked up that rocky path . . . the one I have just come down. And the little pool, Neeka . . . the very same I saw in my dream and those horrible. . . ." He stopped. He would never forget those ugly, hideous shapes scattered about the slopes of this sacred place.

Neeka put her hand on his arm. "Look—there in that dead tree."

Kontu blinked several times, cleaning his thoughts of the bad dream. An eagle, a golden eagle, noblest of birds, father of the Adena people, perched on the stark limb. Out of the corner of his eye Kontu saw Neeka crouch and draw back her throwing arm with the spear poised.

He turned, horrified, "No . . . Neeka! Do not throw . . . Father Eagle! No!"

But he was too late. She took two steps forward and sent

the spear toward the eagle. And then suddenly the spear veered, turned away from the bird and struck the rock wall. Sparks trailed from the flint point, and the spear clattered onto a little ledge.

The eagle rose silently into the air and sailed off over their heads and down the gorge. Neeka watched it out of sight. She looked at Kontu and smiled in her crooked way. "If I believed in such things, I would say some power caused my spear to miss."

Kontu was silent. It had seemed to him also that the spear had been turned aside in a strange sudden way. Perhaps it was a current of air; along the river the winds often blew in odd cross-drafts. Then again, Father Eagle was all powerful. "The Adena people respect Eagle and never kill him," Kontu answered finally. "Yovo would have been frightened if you had killed an eagle on the eve of his journey."

"Almost anything frightens Yovo, one way or another," she answered. "It is good he has a little bag of magic for comfort. Remember that, Kontu, remember. Do not let him become separated from it, for he will die."

She sighed and suddenly looked sad. "He will die perhaps anyway. But I should like him to die in peace, not in the torment he is in now. That is one reason I am leaving. He is a good man and he has been a good priest. But now in his heart he fears that he did the wrong thing letting me travel with you. He will be easier when I have left."

"But there was a sign—" Kontu began and she interrupted swiftly, "Three doves in a summer woods? How could there *not* be such a sign? And look at how misfortune has followed you ever since—storms and ill health and quarrels. And worst of all . . . much worse were the silent gods. They will not speak to him because he has done wrong. They spoke to you, but to him they say nothing. He is afraid and he will be better without me."

She scanned the cliffside looking for a way up. "I am glad I did not kill the eagle. I wanted his feathers. Itza no doubt knows someone who might need them. But I am glad I missed."

"I see your spear, I think," Kontu pointed.

"Probably the point is broken," she grumbled. "You and Yovo can take consolation in that."

They climbed together. Kontu hoped the spear had not been broken. Making such a weapon was hard work, and Neeka would never ask for help from either Gunt or Watota, both of whom were better at flint work than she was.

They climbed. The big stones were warm from the bright sun falling through the budding trees. The lichens on them were green and bright. Kontu liked stretching his legs and arms and climbing up the slippery broken face of the temple hill.

"There," he said, pointing, "there is the end of your spear . . . see it, sticking out from that ledge?"

They climbed a little higher and Neeka scrambled onto the narrow strip of rock. "The spear is here—and with a broken point as I knew," she said. "Kontu, a sort of doorway!" she exclaimed. He saw a narrow opening between boulders. She did not pause. Quickly she squeezed inside and he followed close behind.

They were in a small room and in the dim light they strained to see around them. Water dripped somewhere. They moved cautiously forward and Neeka cried out, "Look! There at the back!"

Kontu peered over her shoulder and saw something tall and white in the crack of dark rock. "A skeleton . . . with a headdress just like Yovo's," she whispered.

Chapter Seventeen

Kontu pushed around her then till he could see for himself. The bones of someone long dead were wedged into a crevice so that the rib cage and skull were still upright, but the other bones, broken, gnawed by mice, lay in a tumble on the floor.

Out of the bare skull grew antlers of copper, on a circlet of copper, a priest's crown, like Yovo's. Kontu drew a deep slow breath. He felt half suffocated with fear and joy and awe. He touched Neeka's arm. He was not sure anything was real, he might be dreaming. He looked at the things on the floor, the pipes, the skull bowl and the sacred tablets— the incised stones which Adena wizards used to mark their bodies for certain ceremonies. And Adena wizards only!

"We must leave," he said slowly. "We must leave here at once and tell Yovo."

Neeka did not answer and he himself did not turn, but merely went on staring, holding onto the girl's arm.

"Are you all right?" she asked finally, her voice was rough, but she was concerned for him, he knew.

"We must leave," he repeated, and she shook his hand from her arm and seized him by the shoulders and shoved him through the tiny portal and out into the light of day. He could not tell if the spring-swollen river roared in his ears or it was his own blood racing. The loud triumphant song he heard might be the song of a bird or it might be his heart singing.

"We must tell Yovo," he mumbled. He had not failed. His dream had led them rightly. This was the place, this was what they searched for! An Adena sorcerer still held power here, still kept watch over a holy place. He sat down suddenly on the ledge before the cave and the world swam and tilted about him. He raised his face to the sun falling softly between the tiny new greenery of a slender tree. Slowly his vision steadied and he saw Neeka watching him, frowning.

"Listen, you with your head made of mud and your knees made of sand," she snapped. "We cannot leave here if you will not walk. We cannot tell Yovo anything if we sit here all day and look at the sky. And I cannot tell Yovo anything for I do not know anything. Were those things in the cave the things of your people once? Were they things you hold sacred?"

Kontu nodded and explained briefly their purposes. But the tablets! He had one himself, given him when he was accepted as an initiate, engraved with an image of a hooked-beaked eagle with sharp talons. On the back were three grooves, for sharpening the tiny flint knife used in this way only. When the knife was honed very fine he gashed his wrist and mixed the blood with paint. The other side of the flat tablet was dipped in the mixture and with it he stamped his body all over, leaving the portrait of Eagle on his skin from ankle to forehead. Such a tablet Yovo had used to stamp his forehead when they went among the traders, so that everyone might know he was a priest.

He explained about the tablets as best he could, stumbling over the words, still dazed and confused. But then he sprang up.

"We must tell Yovo!" he cried for the third time.

"Then go tell him," she answered evenly. "You need not tell him I saw the sacred objects. He would not like it."

Hastily Kontu turned and began to climb down the cliff. She had a right to see the sacred things. It was Neeka who had found the cave, her spear, aimed at Eagle himself, had shown the way. What would Yovo say to that?

He scrambled up the path and over the wall of the Sacred Circle and out the entrance, and ran and ran. Under the hemlocks Yovo sat by the ashes of the morning's fire. He looked almost asleep and started when Kontu stood before him panting and speechless. "What is it?" the old man asked impatiently. "Is something the matter?"

When he was able to talk, Kontu explained what was inside the narrow cave. Yovo questioned him closely about the antler headdress and each of the objects, and then at last was quiet, staring off into the distance so intently that Kontu turned to look too. Surely Yovo saw Eagle flying toward them through the skies?

But no, there were only the feathery spring trees and an occasional cloud. The little river behind their shelter fell down the series of ledges and falls, and the wind carried the chuckling voices away and mingled them with those of a morning gathering of crows. It was a lovely place. No wonder his people had been a good and happy people. No wonder they had left this place reluctantly and had hoped so long to find it again. For this was their old home, he knew now. And surely Yovo knew?

Kontu glanced around at the old sorcerer and Yovo smiled. A kind of light seemed to glow from inside him. His spine seemed to have grown straighter and his head sat proudly on his shoulders, as an eagle's sits.

"Is this the place then?" asked Kontu quietly.

The priest did not answer but asked, "How did you come to find the cave?"

Kontu hesitated. "I did not find it, Father Yovo," he

admitted. "She found it . . . the girl . . . Neeka."

He thought Yovo would be displeased. But the old man seemed delighted. "Kontu, the gods do not fail us if we do as they bid," he cried. "See how your dream told us that we would come to the right place, no matter how many bad things and difficulties might stand in the way. See how the spirits bade me bring the girl with us, though it might have seemed the wrong thing to do. Look how it was that the accident to Gunt's foot kept us here when we might have left. And how Neeka was the one to show us the sacred objects. And now . . . now we have succeeded. Though I have yet received no message, I do believe we have found the Eye in the Forest and the others who took that silly route by water, they have failed. Never forget, Kontu. He who does as the gods would have him do will never be bereft."

"I will always try very hard," Kontu promised. He would try very hard. The gods had sent him a dream and that was a sign that they held him in esteem and he would be a priest. Yovo had said as much. The dream had been a true vision and he, Kontu, had been the means of saving the Adena people. Part of the means.

But something worried him. Had Yovo done something wrong, something that displeased Fire and Snake and To-bacco, Father Eagle himself? All these days and they had kept silent. Yovo had come close to leaving this place be-cause he had had no reason to believe it was the right place. Why had not one of the gods spoken to him?

Perhaps Yovo read the question in his eyes. "The priest," he said, "the ancient priest in the little cave. He is still here and he is still the power, the force, of this place. He is a very High Priest and until his bones are properly buried, he remains the priest here and I am an intruder. The spirits could not reveal themselves to me, only to him. This afternoon I will speak with him, show him that I am capable of taking over his priestly duties, then Snake and Fire and Tobacco will give us final proof that this is indeed the Eye. Then we will ease his bones and possessions into the comforting, restful earth where they have long belonged."

Yovo stood up and put his hand on the boy's shoulder. "I must start my prayers and preparations now. I will use the Wolf ritual, for that comes closest to being my very own. Wolf has seldom failed me."

Kontu nodded. The Adena believed that the best way to reach the gods was through an animal. Wolf was wise, careful, knowing. Yovo too was wise and careful. It would be easy for man and animal to become one and the same. Then those who decided life for the Adena people would listen.

"You must help me at the cave," Yovo told him, "for you are truly a priest and truly the gods have wished you to bring us here to save the Adena."

Kontu bent his head in ackowledgment of the praise. The little brown bird racing along over the rivers sang its wild sweet song, and he recognized it this time as the song his heart might sing. He was so filled with pride and pleasure that it seemed likely his heart might sing.

Yovo did not allow Kontu to accompany him into the Sacred Circle, for this beginning part of the ceremony was very personal when Wolf and the priest must reestablish their friendship and their confidence in each other.

Kontu's part was to sit on the ledge before the cave and shake the rattles and sing and chant and prepare the ancient one inside for the coming ceremony. He reached the cave and looked around. Climbing to the ledge, he sat to one side, cross-legged. Trembling with fear and anticipation, he took a deep breath and began.

The sun passed overhead and sank into the afternoon.

His voice was hoarse from chanting, his arms grew numb from weariness. How he managed to keep shaking the rattles with two such sticks of arms he did not know. But he did. On and on.

Then suddenly there was Wolf at the ledge. Kontu was startled. He had been watching through the trees and rocks, but he had not seen the priest approach. He stopped his chant and let his arms drop. He admired Yovo's wolf mask. The ears stood up, alert and wary, the yellow fangs protruded from the jaws. How fierce it looked, and how strange, with Yovo's eyes far away behind the dark eye-holes of the mask. The robe the old man wore was made of wolf skins and decorated with claws and teeth sewn along the hem so that they clicked when he moved.

Yovo trotted about the ledge and made a gesture to the world that all might see that he was no longer Yovo, but Wolf, who is wise. He spoke loudly and clearly so that the priest in the cave might hear, and the others also. Though Neeka and Gunt and Watota and the traders were not to be seen, Kontu knew that they had come to see what might happen and were hidden nearby.

"Listen, ancient and honored one in the cave. I am Wolf and I speak to you for my friend—the Adena priest, Yovo, who comes here from far away in the north. Listen, and I will tell you why he comes here, why he seeks to talk to you. He has told me and now I tell you. Hear!

"Once the Adena people lived in another place. It was a place of abundance of every sort of food; it was a place of beauty and peacefulness. No foe came near, and when the young men went to war, they brought home many heads of the enemy and strong slaves.

"For this place was watched over by an eye, by an eye of the forest. Night and day it watched and did not close, but guarded our people from year's end to year's end. It looked upon them with love. And they returned this love with great honor, great respect, and did all things as it bade them to do.

"Ages of fathers and sons passed and all was well with the people. But then a bad thing happened. No one knows why it happened or how it happened. But the Eye in the Forest shut, after all those seasons of watching, it closed in sleep.

"It came about this way. The earth shook. It shook a little each day as the moon grew fat, then thinned to nothing, and the sky was red and the air was dark and still. And then one day the earth shook very hard, trees fell and the earth lifted and split apart. Clouds of dust rose into the air and rocks flew as high as the sailing vultures. And then the earth was still again. But the Eye was closed and slept.

"The people were afraid. The priests said they must leave and seek another place to live. And so they did. But before they left that beautiful place which had been their home, it was told to the priests that a day would come when once again the Eye would open. Once again it would look with favor upon the Adena people. And if the people were ever sad and in trouble, then they should seek out the Eye once again. And the Eye in the Forest would open and shine like the sun, and the people's ills would shrivel up as drops of rain would dry away on hot stones."

Wolf paused and all around it was solemn and quiet there on the side of the sacred temple ridge. "O Ancient Priest, that is why Yovo has come here. His people are troubled. They need help. They wish to return here and shelter in the strength and benevolence of the Eye as in former days."

Once again Wolf paused. And this time he turned to face the cave entrance. "I come to plead for Yovo," Wolf spoke. "He is wise in Adena ways. Hand over your powers. Let Yovo be priest here. I, Wolf, come to hear what you say."

Yovo began to chant his Wolf song and slipped into the cave. The song went on and on, and the faint sound of his feet as he danced. Kontu's part was over. He had prepared the Ancient Priest for this meeting, assuring him with his words and rattles there was nothing to fear. He sat there cross-legged, listening tensely.

And then there was a long, deep, wailing howl and Kontu felt the hair move on his scalp, for Yovo was now truly Wolf. A high thin voice broke in querulously and Wolf snapped and snarled and Yovo sang, echoes flew in and out of the cave, the voices all spoke at once, and Kontu was afraid. The voices rose to a crescendo and suddenly silence fell and after a long moment Yovo spoke, Kontu could hear his voice but could not make out the words.

The thin high fleshless voice of the dead priest answered. Three times the dead magician and the living one questioned and answered. Kontu knew the others were pressing close to hear, standing below him in the deepening shadows of the afternoon.

Then Kontu almost threw his rattles, almost fell off the ledge, almost screamed. For out of the cave without warning rolled the bare yellow skull. It stared up at the sky out of its empty eye sockets and its thin half-screaming voice cried, "This is the Eye in the Forest! The Adena Eye!"

And at once Yovo appeared from the cave, wearing the time-greened copper antlers.

"It is the Eye!" he said.

Chapter Eighteen

Neeka had gathered roots, long crinkly ones with leaves and white flowers and small round ones with grasslike stems, to flavor the rabbit stew. It smelled very good steaming in the ashes. Itza especially seemed to enjoy it.

"In my travels I eat many kinds of foodstuffs," he said. "One gets to like variety. You Adena seem too easily pleased, to me. Snakes and snails! But this stew is very good. These little roots bite back when they are bitten." He chewed vigorously. "Once a trader gave me a little red pod brought far from the south, he said it was used to flavor food. I was curious and bit it. Oh, what a fire burned in my mouth and throat. Water could not put it out, no matter how much I drank. Tears rolled down my cheeks—I wept like a child."

Watota laughed uproariously. He had known all along that this big fellow with his dotted face was really not brave at all, could be made to cry by a mere plant pod. Itza joined in good-naturedly and Neeka smiled.

A bat skittered down over the fire and then up into the deepening blue of twilight, and in the distance the voices of countless frogs rose up in a glad welcome to warm weather. An owl snarled and Watota quickly hushed his laughter.

He never liked the cries of owls. There was nothing evil

about an owl if it was really a bird, but one could never tell when an owl was truly a bird and when it was an evil spirit in disguise. In the morning he and Gunt would be beginning a long arduous journey, beset with dangers. He did not like to hear the owl call.

Kontu knew what Watota was thinking. He was himself not at all worried. There were three priests here, one of them of such enormous powers that he could do magic many long years after his death. No evil spirit would dare come near.

He was not worried or afraid but he was sad. For now they all sat around the campfire, eating a hot meal, cheerful and laughing. But tomorrow there would be only Kontu and Yovo, alone in the forest, surviving as best they could. Tomorrow the other five would set out together. Gunt and Watota would travel with the traders for several days, for Itza had promised to show them the best and fastest path to the northern country of their home. When they reached that path, Gunt and Watota would go one way, Neeka and the two traders another. And Yovo and Kontu would be left alone, to hope that the warriors soon reached the Adena country with the good news of their discovery, and hurried back with the High Priest and a villageful of people to see the marvel; left alone, to eat snails and snakes and to wonder what would become of Neeka.

Itza would fare well with his helper, Kontu was sure of that. But what of Neeka and her strange ways and her sharp tongue? He wished she would not go. But then what would she do when the others arrived from the northern towns? They would not understand her.

He was still thinking about it when he lay down on his pallet. The last thing he saw was a red glow of coals as Yovo lit his pipe, to ask Tobacco to look kindly on all of them in the days to come.

He awoke early, as a priest should do, of his own accord. Yovo was stirring about and so was Gunt. The pale sky shone through the branches of trees as Kontu walked to the river. When he came from his prayer-bath, Gunt was there on the bank. He stood in a froth of blue flowers, looking down at them.

"How lucky we are that the gods decided to give us flowers, they are so beautiful," he said suddenly.

Kontu was surprised. He had not thought of such a thing. Gunt bent and touched one of them gently. As he straightened up, Kontu saw he was carrying a fishnet. "I thought I would try to leave you some fish; I have had no luck hunting these last few days."

Watota had been more successful, but that meat they would carry with them when they left. Gunt was a better fisher than hunter anyway, by far.

"That would please us," answered Kontu.

Gunt did not move. He stood looking at the flowers and at length he said quietly, "All my life I have asked nothing more than to be able to sit and look. The world is always beautiful if one really looks."

Kontu supposed that was so, but he thought it was a strange thing for Gunt to say to him. Anyway, no one could simply sit and look, not all the time. Everyone had to hunt or help in the fields or go to war or be a priest.

Gunt walked slowly away through the rocks, and did not seem to be looking at anything. He climbed across a flat rock where the water splashed up continually as the river fell into a deep pool below. The rock was mossy and slippery; Gunt was so awkward.

Suddenly Kontu cried out. "Be careful, Gunt, careful!" he called.

Gunt simply raised his hand—and then he was gone.

Kontu shrieked and ran to the river's edge. In the clear

water he saw the strong current grab at Gunt and carry the thick body over the edge of the pool and down among the rocks and whirl it away and away and down and down.

It was past noon and all of them were tired from scrambling up and down the riverbank looking for Gunt. Watota wished to wait for the morning before they began their journey. He did not like that things had commenced so badly and he did not like the fact that he would have to make the journey alone for the most part. But Itza was ready and eager to travel. He knew the other traders were gathered at their meeting place. If Watota reached this spot in time, he could probably find one of the merchants who might accompany him most of the way to the Adena towns, Itza argued.

Yovo too thought that further delay would not be a good thing. Everything was prepared, the protection he had asked from the gods for Watota and Gunt on this pilgrimage would go with Watota, no matter what had befallen Gunt.

Kontu wished they would stay another night. He knew it was a selfish wish, not becoming to a priest. But the sight of Gunt falling into the water had troubled him deeply, in his mind he saw it over and over. There had been something strange about it, the last words Gunt had said to him and the way he had gone out on the rocks, which he had well known to be treacherous, along a river perilously swift and swollen. It was not like Gunt, who had spent much time along the little streams and learned their wicked ways.

Neeka said suddenly, "Little Brother, it is not a cause for great grief. He liked it here. He will be happy."

Once again she had said something that horrified Kontu. How could Gunt be happy lying far from home drowned in some green pool? It was true he had not been happy in the Adena village, teased and tormented, made to feel a fool, when all he asked was to be allowed to sit and look. But he had been at home, where even fools had their place. Kontu stared at the girl. He could not make her understand. Yovo might be able to do so with patience, to make her see that in a village all must take part, that it was better to be nothing and suffer the consequences, than to be nothing and lost forever, separate and apart from everything that mattered, gone without the priestly rites that would assure Gunt's spirit the peace of the after-realms of the Dark Land of Forever.

Kontu wished he was wise, so that he could tell her of these things. But perhaps it was useless to try. She was Neeka and everything about her was unlike everything about other people. And the proof, if he needed proof, was the swift impatient way she made ready to leave. She could hardly wait to go. He could see that she could hardly wait, scarcely bear it when Yovo stood before them and intoned a prayer, ending with his blessing: "May Father Eagle clear the briers from your path and turn your feet from peril."

"Live in Eagle's shadow," responded Itza and Watota, for that is the proper response. But Neeka made no answer, only pivoted abruptly and walked away. The others followed. Yovo and Kontu watched. Surely she would turn and wave. One of them would turn and wave. But the travelers walked steadily on, and by and by were lost to sight. . . . Later that day Kontu found her pot, filled with the little flavorful roots and some dried meat, left where he would be sure to find it. She had, after all, said good-bye.

The Ancient Priest must be buried, that was the first thing to do. Although he had delivered his power into Yovo's hands, until he was suitably buried he was still there and that was not good. He must be allowed to enter the world of the spirits as quickly as possible.

The earth was soft and Kontu had no trouble digging the grave with a stick. Yovo, following the old old ritual, gathered bark in a special way to line the grave. With the stone ax Kontu cut the saplings which would be laid across the body and made a heap of flat stones to be placed on top of the little trees.

There were songs and prayers as they fetched the yellow bones and the priest's possessions to the graveside and laid them on the bark. The graveside blaze was lit and Red Fire was invoked and red paint scattered over the skeleton, the saplings laid across the body and then the stones. Dark sweet-smelling earth was heaped over it all, and now the venerable one was with his people in the Dark Land of Forever.

Very close by Yovo laid Gunt's weapons, his spear and throwing stick, his knife and his grass sack of trinkets, and these too he buried with all ceremony. Even if Gunt's body was never recovered, surely such an old and powerful priest would watch over his soul and see that it came to no harm but was provided with all it needed.

That night with Yovo, Kontu smoked the Two-Legged Sacred Breath, the pipe carved like a small deformed man. "You are a true priest now," Yovo said, "for you have taken part in the most sacred of all ceremonies, the beginning of a burial mound that brings life to its circling end and its beginning. If I should die before our people arrive here, bury me there. You . . . you will be the priest and tend the Sacred Fire. All alone. You will have to be the Adena priest and the Adena people." It was a pleasing and terrifying thought. It made Kontu's heart race and his head swim and the tobacco almost choked him.

He slept late the next day, but Yovo slept late too and

did not scold him. The day before had been long and tiring, the old man moved slowly and shakily on his way to the river. But Kontu, though he missed the others, had never felt so strong and happy and confident. He wished he might run and scream and leap about and laugh and roll in the warm sun, like a four-year-old. But such things were not becoming to a priest.

Instead he walked sedately inside the walls of the temple, crossing the wide field of young trees to look at the Sacred Eye, the Eye in the Forest, which he had himself discovered in a dream.

How green the moss was, and the new grass! The small flowers sparkled in the early sun and he looked at them carefully, remembering Gunt's words. In a little while he came to the pupil of the Eye, the small bright pool in whose far depths the clear waters boiled out of the earth and on whose surface lay only the blue sky.

Kontu stared down past the reflections to the very bottom, where the little spring sent up its purling fountain, not into the air but into its own transparent water. The Eye was open and would never close again. His dream had brought them to this place and it would be theirs always and the bad part of the dream was over and gone—the sky darkened and he looked up but there were no clouds, only that terrible foul-smelling ugly haze smothering the earth's circle. And there around him were the blasted trees, misshapen and diseased. And there again the monstrous things, with their strange and dreadful rufous fungus.

He walked slowly forward and put out his hand on one of the things, fearfully. What a hard cold scaly cover it had under the crust, so that it could never rot and die the way other things did but must lie forever under the horrible sky, under the hunched and broken trees, amid all that repulsive, scarred, and loathsome landscape.

The vision went, as it had gone before. But Kontu knew

suddenly that Yovo was wrong. The bad part of his dream had not been obstacles that stood in their way to finding the Eye in the Forest. The bad part was a prophecy of what could happen to a sacred place.

It could happen. . . . How could it happen? The Adena people would not make it happen; they were a good people, who did what the gods bade them to do. But there were other people, people like the Primitives. Like Itza, who believed in everything, or pretended to believe, and like Neeka, who believed in nothing. And even among the Adena, there were those who were not happy, who felt themselves deserted by the gods. He had seen it himself; he had seen Gunt go into the water, and in his heart he knew it had been deliberate. He knew Gunt could not go back to a life where there was no real place for him, though he was one of the Adena. . . . It could happen.

Kontu shivered in the warm sun. No, no, he cried silently, it shall not happen! Could he keep it from happening? What could he do? He was a priest; a priest could surely keep it from happening. Something inside him said, It will happen. It could happen. A priest could do what he could, do everything that he believed the spirits wished him to do, be strong and give his people wisdom and help them to be courageous. But some things he could not change, could not prevent.

Was there no other thing he could do? He closed his eyes and asked Eagle what he might do.

He could be happy. He opened his eyes and looked around, at pink bushes blooming along the walls and the gold and orange of the oak tassels and the sudden new greenery of wild plums. He heard the wind rustle the grass and the distant sounds of the rivers and the sweet voices of birds. He smelled the fragrance of wet clean earth.

He could be happy!

Authors' Note

The story told in these pages is purely fictional. It has only a most tenuous basis in fact.

An early governor of Ohio named his estate, which included Indian mounds, Adena. When one of these mounds was excavated, the name Adena was given to the people whose artifacts were discovered there. Since that first excavation, many other burial mounds of these people have been dug into and quite a bit is known about them. However, much is also unknown, and much about the uses of certain artifacts is pure surmise. The dates given for the Adena culture are arbitrary, but that it existed from about 1,000 B.C. to perhaps A.D. 100 seems a reasonable guess.

It is generally agreed that the Adena people in the Ohio River valley developed the "first extensive burial cult, built the first substantial homes, made some of the earliest ceramics and practiced (early) agriculture" among the North American Indians.

The earthworks called the Old Stone Fort at Manchester, Tennessee, bears some resemblance to sacred circles in the Ohio River region. It is known to have been constructed before the Adena culture vanished, but at a time when those people were evidently hard-pressed and about to be swallowed up by other populations.

It is possible that some of the Adena were forced out of the Ohio region and came south to the Tennessee River valley, though this too is disputed. Recent archaeological investigations of the Old Stone Fort give no reason to suppose Adena used this sacred circle, but it could be. A secret cave on the side of the ridge below the sacred walls was once mentioned in a newspaper article, but it has not been located. No Adena tablets have been found on the site, or bones of an Adena burial, though it is conceivable they are there, waiting to be uncovered.

Otherwise the cultural ways and the material objects mentioned in this book are taken from suggestions and finds from Adena burial mounds made by anthropologists.